THE TOWERS OF METROPOLIS

The Towers of Metropolis Volume 2
"And Metropolis is Paralyzed, Motionless" © 2024 Dexter Fabi
"A Serpent in the Garden of Eternity" © 2024 Carson Demmons
"Movers of the Earth" © 2024 Harding McFadden
"The Secret Army" © 2024 Gary Lovisi

Published by Airship 27 Productions
www.airship27.com
www.airship27hangar.com

Interior and cover illustrations © 2024 James Lyle

Editor: Ron Fortier
Associate Editor:Gordon Dymowski
Marketing and Promotions Manager: Michael Vance
Production Designer: Rob Davis

ISBN: 978-1-953589-71-2

Printed in the United States of America

10 9 8 7 6 5 4 3 2 1

THE TOWERS OF
METROPOLIS
VOLUME TWO
TABLE OF CONTENTS

AND METROPOLIS IS PARALYZED, MOTIONLESS

DEXTER FABI

Tracks all through the night into the city, elevated above, ever winding, ever flowing to the city of industry, the city of the elite. His train car was the dustiest of all, yet his excitement blinded him to the squalor. He felt the direct bumps of the ride on the lowest berth. He had to escape, to immerse himself into the gargantuan city, to merge into something much larger so he could feel anonymous. Anything could happen to him in Metropolis, and it still would have been better than what he was leaving behind.

"Leave it all behind, start anew," he whispered to himself as the train careened at bullet speed towards the largest city on earth, a city of fifty-five million inhabitants.

Intruding on his exhilarated thoughts of the future were the stories of the workers below the city and how he could avoid becoming one of them. If he ingratiated himself to the indulgent ways of the people aboveground, to further their lifestyles in any capacity, no matter how low or menial the job was, then he could survive. It was his choice to live a life where he would become a new person. A new home was all he was looking for to take care of the sting of the past.

All he had with him was a battered suitcase, a dream, his wits, and seventeen Metropolis paper notes for money. He clutched onto all his belongings as the train entered the flashing city of myriads of blinking windows and spires that touched the sky.

✛✛✛

Towers upon spires, upon spires on towers, as limitless as the limited eye could see. His train rushed through the supreme wonder of the world, the city of Metropolis, its lights winking and shimmering in the early night. Through the window of his train car, he could see the rush of the crowd streams, the hectic flow of the arteries of the city. The city was a concrete garden of otherworldly delights. It was a vast playground, the mother city of the globe, a city where every vice was indulged and those who worked below in the depths

5

of the city were ignored. Metropolis was always awake, a city that flowed at a constant and methodical hurry at all dials of the clock.

After the train, he had taken a taxi to where he had responded in an advertisement, a tenement in one of the beaten areas of Metropolis. For him, it was a start, a foothold.

Displayed outside on his ride to the apartment building's address was more than anyone could process visually. There were stratoscrapers so soaring as if to be built by demigods, superstructures with rows, columns, and diagonals of lighted windows adding to the collective luminosity, spectaculars advertising Eranot, Daviosan, and Utamoh. Tickers proclaimed the latest news in lights as it scrolled on apparatuses on elevated freeways. Billions of lights flickered as searchlights arced wide through the sky, surging. He was in the city that embodied the ultimate peak of civilization.

He had also responded to an ad for employment found in the Metropolis Courier newspaper, to be a lantern bearer in the Yoshiwara, a club that catered to the city's nobility. It wasn't much, but he knew that at least he wouldn't be driven below into the Workers' City. The employment was confirmed as he had fit what they were looking for. Till that first paycheck arrived from simply holding an Eastern lantern while wearing outlandish attire in a club of the jet set, he knew that he had to eat minimally, force himself to meagre sustenance. What worried him was that he might have to go hungry if he didn't have enough till his first payday. Even so, he was prepared for anything, as he was glad to be there in this teeming city with its seemingly endless citizens.

The cab had brought him to a wretched building behind a row of five story constructions facing west. Exiting the cab, he took his first deep breath of the Metropolis air, taking out the key that was sent when he signed up for the apartment.

He now had fifteen Metropolis notes after the cab ride. Stepping onto the ruptured pavement, his foot had caught a flier for an event near Yoshiwara and the night spot district. He brought the sullied flier up and put it into his jacket pocket to look at later because he was eager to see his living arrangements. He had agreed to the apartment, sight unseen. It had taken all of his life savings. It was a risk he was willing to venture, even if it entailed a bleak financial situation. His job would begin in a week and he'd be back on his feet. He would have to stretch out what he had left till then.

The elevator inside was permanently so he had to take seven flights of stairs to get to his door. Inside the building were cobwebbed and dingy walls. Almost breathless from the climb and walking on the worn threads of the hall carpets, he found his door and turned his key.

What he saw was about what he was expecting, according to the ad: small, and yet, this kind of small was a slight shock to him. Definitely a case of false advertising.

As to furniture, there was one table, a chair with a lean to it, a floor mattress, two plates, a fork, a spoon, and an inexplicable nightstand. The view from the one window showed two trees and a grubby lot in the foreground. It was the background view that made up for the foreground, a remote evening lightshow of Metropolis: a configuration of neon lights on levels, grids of urban sprawl in a beautifully ordered pattern. Nonstop cars in their snaky lines of traffic added to the winking cityscape. As he looked, he searched for the Metropolis Stadium where the Sons of the City had their games of track and field. Finding the stadium, a discernible speck, he thought that he would like to visit it when he had a chance. The New Tower of Babel was easy to locate as it rose the highest into the sky above all, the iconic structure signifying the importance of the city, a city for otherworldly architects. The other cities of the world imitated themselves after this city, but they could not come close to the level of this sprawling megalopolis of immense pagoda-like structures and feats of architecture that ensorcelled the eye.

Turning his view back to the cramped and lonely apartment, he heaved a sigh and took a clean bed sheet from his suitcase to put on the mattress on the floor. More dust for him to contend with floated upwards from the mattress. It seemed that dust assailed him since the journey to Metropolis, but he did not let it get to him. He sat on the mattress, breathed in deeply again and began to meditate. Soon, a form of tranquility prevailed, and after a while, he opened his eyes and looked again on his new home.

"We all have to start somewhere, and I'm just glad that I'm not one of those underground," he reassured himself.

He hung his jacket on the asymmetric chair and proceeded to make sure that all he brought with him in his jacket pockets was still there. Accounting for all he had, he drew the flier from his pocket as he settled into the chair and read by the pulsing glow of the city.

An evening of dance was being promoted on the flier, to be held at the night spot Frothland, the large letters distorted. A phrase was on the flier, "If you wish to be loved, then love," attributed to Seneca, along with silhouettes of svelte human figures in depicted foam and lather, the proclaimed entrance fee being ten Metropolis notes.

He looked at what he had left. If anything, he liked to take chances, and he would have to subsist on even more austere eating if he went. Besides, it was the first night of the rest of his new Metropolitan life.

He decided to go, taking possibility by the winds. The event was not till later in the evening so he slept on the mattress on the floor for an hour, then briefly glanced at the damaged ceiling before heading to the mingy bathroom.

After waiting for the rust to run through the pipes, he washed all the dust from the train into the city off and sought his best clothing for an evening on the town. He made sure to check himself in the mirror. Sure, he didn't look like most inhabitants of the aboveground Metropolis, but he was still satisfied with how he looked before becoming one with the night. In the fractured mirror, he smiled for the first time in weeks.

✝✝✝

Passing through Metropolis's renowned "Club of the Sons," a district meant as a watering ground for the Sons of those who controlled the city, he tried to evade throngs of people embracing the night. For a while, he looked at the building that centered in the district, the actual Club of the Sons, one of the most resplendent buildings in all Metropolis. He had never seen such architecture before, so perfect in symmetry, so calculated to the very centimeter to produce ultimate aesthetic delight.

While walking in a hypnotic state around the district, he viewed its library, its picture-palaces, its lecture-rooms, its opulent theatres. The library was open, and while the keepers of the library looked at him a bit more, he was allowed, along with most visitors to Metropolis, to view the Club of the Sons Library on a guided tour.

This library held all of the world's books that have been printed. He gazed with a sense of staggering awe at the collection—volumes on volumes, a museum of the world's literature. Circulation was limited to the Sons as there were rare books, precious in each existence. Looking at the titles from afar as he was led around by one of the evening docents in a group of other library visitors, he had read many spines, lurid titles and some scholarly titles, all tantalizing to him. The Sons' Library was meant more as a bragging piece than for the public's actual benefit, a flashy bauble to prove that the fathers of Metropolis wanted the best for the Sons of the city.

After the library, he mused on the Stadium, impossible to miss. It was closed and only viewable from the outside. He dreamt of the tracks within, how the Sons were given the best of everything that life could offer. He also thought of the exterior of the "Eternal Gardens," the renowned paradise kept also for the Sons, a place where they frolicked in their carefree and protected lives filled with personal servants to fulfill their every beck and whim. The milky color of the glass ceiling of the Gardens shone like a black opal in the night, the searchlights of the city glinting off it from time to time, pronouncing its beauty for all to see.

Already he was beginning to alleviate himself of his former life. His best suit of clothes, though worn-out and with holes in places, looked dashing to those who saw him. As eyes roved onto him, he felt that these evening faces could gather that he was new to the city. He tried to hide that he was frantically looking for street signs, furtively looking at them from afar or from corners of his vision.

Peals of laughter and frivolity rang through the night. The masses that walked by, in brocade, in velvet, in papyrus, in all manner of clothing that spelled of luxury or otherwise, passed by in a kaleidoscopic blur. Cloche hats and cupid bow lips. The aromas of rotgut moonshine and bootleg gin on the nighttime populace. Cars of the likes he had never seen sped in a haze, one instance of the automobile stream with a lady driver racing a jewel of a car against the gentlemen who also raced with her. Some of the people of the night wore excesses of cellophane, some of it shockingly see-through, leaving nothing and everything to the imagination. Some managed to wear paper, mint-colored and delicate, waving in the artificial breezes made by the incessant trains as they roared by. It seemed that those who were wearing paper outfits wanted them to be torn by the artificial breezes or that they wore them as a dare to themselves to see how long the paper clothing would last the night.

In contrast to the denizens of the night, he saw the workers of the machine-city for the first time. Clothed in dark blue linen, hard shoes, and black caps, their faces never carried the smiles of those clearly enjoying the decadences of the evening. Their heads were always looking at the ground, walking in ordered rows, blocks of them trudging in a tired, heavy step, synchronous with each other. He observed that they marched in metronome time to a clock that only they could hear. And when they were called to their shifts by the loud whistle that blasted through the city every ten hours, splitting the ears of everyone in Metropolis, they descended underground to a fate that only made him shiver.

It reminded him of his life back home, his former life now. It all seemed so strange that just two days ago he was plowing in his field, the earth unyielding due to insufficient rainfall, the dryness of the ground causing chaos in the village, and the drinking water in the village contaminated, leaving several he knew dead or damaged permanently.

Still in a daze at the jubilation of the city night and overlooking his stomach rumbling, he found himself outside the Club of the Sons district and felt that he was nearing Frothland. The wheels of this machine-city pulsated, the planes flew above him in concentric and widening circles, the lifeblood of the city frantic and lighting up the night to proclaim that this was the center of all the seven continents of earth. And for him, this city was where it would happen, this was the canvas where his dreams would come true, the canvas of everything.

✝✝✝

At the entrance to Frothland, he realized he was in a district of the city a few levels below the main levels, though the frivolous atmosphere had not stopped. Twice along the way to his destination for the evening, he was propositioned by pomegranate-mouthed and painted faced citizens. He brushed off their advances, not wanting to ingratiate himself just yet to strangers whom he barely knew. What he wanted instead of instant gratification was conversation, to make his first friend in this city pulsing with the souls of fifty-five million people.

Frothland almost rivalled the entrance to the Club of the Sons. Ravishingly decorated, the doorways were iridescent glass carved with the thousand eyes of doves and owls.

He reached this doorway and handed the entrance fee, not regretting his steady determination to at least connect cerebrally with someone, even if it meant sacrifice and impoverishment for some days.

Entering the premises, Frothland had fulfilled its title—suds and froth were swaying in the air, descending on the patrons and all who gathered there. There must have been hundreds of people enmeshed on a floor, dancing to the hypnotic clash and tranquil beat of unearthly music interspersed with bare hints of jazz. It was music he had never heard before, the crowd seeming to be in the liminal area between the dream and waking world, moving in their unique ways. The bubbles from the suds at times obscured his vision entirely as he led himself sometimes blindly to the floor where everyone created a collective undulation. Already he felt that he had been touched by an anonymous hand, whether intentionally or by accident, he could not place.

A wry smile graced his face. The energy in the air lifted his spirits. As he took to the floor, moving and gyrating in time to the music, he realized that as soon as he started to move, to close his eyes and move along, he let himself be carried in a sort of trance. The movements of the people were influencing his own motions, people from various walks of life all hypnotized and drawn, impelled to dance as if possessed.

The froth had descended on the crowd in waves, blocking other people's vision at times, and he wondered if his clothes would be affected. As the suds of soap landed on his best clothing, he realized that they left no residue at all. The masses of bubbles moved as his whole being was given to the music.

After dancing for a while, he joined the people in the balconies who were watching the enthralling motion of the crowd on the main floor.

As he was watching, he noticed the other people in the premises. Not as flashy as the people in the Sons' District, he could tell that they were having a good time among the bevies of suds that cascaded through the air. Some of them were inevitably capturing them with their hands and blowing them on the people that they arrived with. While watching, he too captured some of the soapy froth and held it in his hands, having the feel of real suds that miraculously left no residue.

"First time at Frothland, isn't it?" piped a voice near to him.

He turned to the source of the voice, distinctive as its sound waves carried above the loud music.

It was a young lady dressed in a headband of silvery shimmer and a dress as slate gray as the sky after a summer thunderstorm.

"You have the look. I had the same look the first time I saw Frothland too. What's your name?" she asked, her voice still clear in spite of the entrancing music.

"My name's Sovann, what's yours?" he said as his hand extended.

She gladly took his hand and said that her name was Thandiwe.

"Nice to meet you, Sovann. Are you new to the city?"

To this, he answered in the affirmative. Was it that obvious? He pondered if all new people to the town had a look that gave away their fresh-to-the-city status.

He smiled, and she smiled back.

"Well, anyway, let's dance," she said as she started to walk away, the crowd enfolding her as she went. Sovann immediately trailed and caught up to her in the press of the people and the suds surging from the above vents.

"I like what you're wearing," she said as more lathers partially blocked his vision. He was embarrassed at the holes and the worn condition of his clothing, but the froth had masked these.

"Who needs a mirror," he replied well enough so she could hear.

They had talked for a while, dancing very near to each other, both relishing the night. Sovann was glad to have company and someone to talk to for the evening. While there were others that had come alone to Frothland, he knew from the looks of them that they were seasoned dwellers of Metropolis.

While in the middle of a long section of subconscious-inducing music, Sovann felt himself to be in the right place. He had only arrived with the intention of making at least one new friend in the city, and it seemed that his new friend was to be Thandiwe.

"Where do you work?" she asked, both of them in time with the music.

"I'll begin work in a couple of days at Yoshiwara. You know, as one of the lantern bearers."

"Yoshiwara! Now that's just wonderful!" she exclaimed.

Just then, an incongruous sound layered onto the music. It was the whistle that ear-splitted the city of Metropolis, signifying that the current shift was over and the new shift for the workers was to begin. It happened every ten hours. Sovann knew what it was, and he trembled.

"After a while you become acclimated to it," said Thandiwe. "Yoshiwara, my, what a placement that is," she said, changing the subject. "So exclusive. The Sons of the Fathers in tuxedos, tinsel and confetti everywhere, the gentry of the city all packed into one glorious night spot. I must admit, I'm envious." They were getting closer and closer as the evening drew on, and soon they were holding each other, two souls in a city of fifty-five million, the population increasing as Metropolitan time went by.

In the course of the evening, Thandiwe had wanted to visit Sovann's apartment, but she said that duty was calling her. She had to go to work in just about four hours from now.

She gave him her calling card, letting him know the numbers to dial for a televideophone call. He was up front and said that he was short on funds till his first paycheck from Yoshiwara. She instructed him to call with the option that she would pay for it. He agreed to do so.

"I really don't like to go, but I'm dedicated to my job. I also work, catering to the Daughters of the Fathers here. As long as I cater and pamper them, and fulfill every petty request they have, I won't be sent underground. You know how it is."

He nodded. He put her card in his jacket pocket.

"Don't forget to call, mein leibling," she said as she went away to get ready for work. "Do you promise?"

"I promise," he replied.

"I'm available the next two days after work."

"Okay, Thandiwe. Then I'll see you tomorrow and the day after that."

He stared at her eyes, her altered golden-flecked eyes, and tried to search, to read, what she was thinking. Without preamble, he moved his face closer, at first giving a small kiss on the mouth. Seeing her subtle delight at this, he gave her a deeper kiss. Thandiwe closed in, her arms drawing him nearer. He didn't withhold affection as his heart was emblazoned, but he also knew at the same time that he must protect his heart. Taking his chances his first night in the city had given a good return. As she walked out, he felt only slightly broken. Each of them waved repeatedly as the other blurred in the distance.

+++

Auburn colored dawn was decorating the eastern side of the city as Sovann walked all the way home. He felt that he was dancing on air.

He came back from his reveries and good feelings suddenly and harshly when he entered his apartment and changed clothes.

The card had vanished.

He searched every pocket multiple times. Still, he couldn't find it. He looked to see if there were any substantial holes in his pockets where a calling card could slip through. None of the holes were big enough for a card of that size to fall out.

Sovann quickly put on the same suit of clothing he wore for his night at Frothland and retraced his steps, running the whole while. Still, he could not find Thandiwe's card.

Sauntering in a somber way to his building, he collapsed onto the front steps. His head cradled in his hands, he began to weep for a connection made and just as soon vanished. Sovann knew it was illogical to fall for someone whose company he only had for about five hours. Yet, the thought of never feeling her skin, seeing her entire presence, never experiencing her embraces again felt as if someone had torn his heart open. The loneliness of this big city was starting to be even more pronounced.

He thought he would search for Thandiwe. He couldn't find any listings in the Metropolis televideophone books for this name. He asked at Frothland if anyone knew a woman by the name of Thandiwe, also giving her description. The workers at Frothland and the higher ups didn't recognize the name and Sovann's description of her.

Sovann busied himself to remedy his heartache, familiarizing himself to his new city. He rode the elevator with its open front door to the observation deck of the New Tower of Babel. He visited the ivory temples of Moloch, Baal, Huitzilopochtli, and Durgha. He visited museums whose collections were the envy of the world and spoke of Metropolis's wealth. Whatever was free as a visitor to the city, he took it, absorbing more about his newfound home. Most of the time, he just contemplated on how beautiful the city was, its futuristic buildings crowded close and altogether beguiling. The city of the future's future, the city of tomorrow's tomorrow.

On each exploratory trip, he looked for her. Of all of the people, none of

...the city of tomorrow's tomorrow.

them were Thandiwe.

He felt a sense of relief when his first day of work at Yoshiwara arrived. Sovann at last could focus on something else and forget the misery of a love surprisingly found and then promptly vanished. He was also down to two Metropolis notes so a looming payday was gladly anticipated.

The staff that oversaw Yoshiwara was meticulous. They had put him in beautiful Eastern attire of embroidered silk and had him stand for hours above one of the staircases holding one of the elegant Nipponese paper lamps on a bendable pole. That was all that was required for this job. There were several other employees who had the same role as lantern bearers. They all stood systematically arranged and in the same kind of garment he wore. They were there to add to the ambience, to transport the Sons and their entourages and those who reveled in the night at Yoshiwara with hints of the magnificent Far East.

A lightning storm was raging outside Yoshiwara but it did not prevent the gentry from arriving. There the Sons were, naively clothed in their snowy silken garments, and there were the gentlemen of the club in their tuxedoes, vests, and starched collars. The women that had come to Yoshiwara were always expensively arrayed with their scintillating headbands, feathered headwear, and diamond encrusted upper arm bands scintillating.

A few more months of this stationary holding of a lantern just for show and he would find his way to the next job. Till then, Yoshiwara as a lantern holder would do.

+++

It was months till he established himself in the city. He had friends, fellow lantern holders, that he made at his job. It was through talking to the regulars at Yoshiwara that he learned about the night watchman position at the New Tower of Babel. The position wasn't advertised or public knowledge, but he thought he would apply anyway.

Since their night watchman had recently just disappeared from the job, Sovann was offered the position right away. The timing was perfect. It certainly was more interesting than his job at Yoshiwara, and there wasn't much to do besides living at the topmost level of the Tower and performing regular maintenance duties. It was dangerous, as strong winds could blow about anyone from the Tower if they were not careful. The rumor was that the recent night watchman that vanished was blown clean off the tower by a forceful wind. In spite of this, Sovann knew that he'd take extra precaution. The staff reassured that they would intensify the safety measures. His responsibilities included tending the lights at the very apex of the Tower, oiling and winding the clockwork mechanisms encased there when needed, restocking fuel, and cleaning the lenses of the searchlights. This job was during the late hours of early morning to dawn. The air at that level of the stratosphere was thin and difficult to breathe. For this, he was given a gas mask that made optimal use of the oxygen at that altitude. He was also given a pair of graviton boots that he was instructed to wear to prevent any unplanned falls due to strong winds.

He was restricted from conversing with Jurgen Fredersen, the Brain of Metropolis, whose office was near the lordliest height of the Tower. They had given Sovann the night watchman's quarters and was sent basic food. In the daytime, he could go to the ground levels and was allowed to wander, but during his shift he was bound to stay. He could no longer go to Frothland or any other place of the night, being confined to the Tower's overnight duties.

The view from the foremost height of the New Tower of Babel was exquisite, godlike. Such a sudden and, for his case, welcome change. He could never have forecasted this. Though his wages were modest and the situation dangerous with thin oxygen and unpredictable gusts of wind that could send him over the very edges, it still was an improvement over what he was making at Yoshiwara. The priceless view in itself was worth it. He wondered how many citizens of Metropolis had the right to see what he saw, the loftiest view in the world.

✚✚✚

Sovann, ten months into his duties as the night watchman of the sky-grazing New Tower of Babel, woke one morning, outside on the top of the Tower in the open. His legs felt a bit cramped because the graviton boots plastered him horizontally to the deck since he was lying on his side. He found it passing strange that he woke up away from his bed in the night watchman's quarters and was here outside instead.

He peeled off his gas mask and quickly put it back on due to a current interval of thinness in the air. There was no wind at the moment. The city was eerily quiet. All he could hear was birdsong, music gracing a vista that seemed illogically still.

He took a look at the pocket watch attached to the watch chain on his vest. It had stopped at 3:17 a.m.

Shaking the watch to get it moving, it still was at a dead stop. He felt that he would have to buy a new one.

He saw the other clocks at his height of the Tower. They all told the same time: 3:17 a.m.

The incredible view of Metropolis at that height showed him the pathways of the cars and the trains as well. Nothing was moving. Everything was at a grinding halt. He could hear no roar, no accumulation of the noise of all who lived here. From his vantage point on the Tower, he could see the flying machines of the city and they too were suspended as if parked in midair.

Rubbing his eyes as if he were in a dream, he swiftly realized that he wasn't in the midst of one.

Deciding not to panic just yet, he took the elevator down, even though he was forbidden to speak with Jurgen Fredersen, the Master of Metropolis who ran the city, and his young son, Joh.

There stood Jurgen Fredersen in his office, also with a grand view of the city through his gigantic windows, a tableau surveying his masterwork. It was so silent that Sovann could still hear birdsong, and that was all he heard.

He opened the door to the office and entered softly, knocking tactfully, hushfully.

"Mr. Fredersen? Mr. Fredersen?" Sovann called, trying to deliver it in his most respectful way, a mere croak since he knew he was forbidden to address him or even look him in the eyes directly.

There was no answer. Mr. Fredersen was frozen in place, his hand in the air as he looked at the master view. The blue plate where Fredersen placed his hand upon to signal the workers to go underground was there, untouched.

He could only see Fredersen's back, standing still in place. All the clock faces showed the same time of 3:17 a.m. He moved to look around to where he could see Fredersen's front, all the while wondering if he would get into grave trouble by addressing Mr. Fredersen.

Cautiously moving, he beheld the cold, unfeeling visage of Mr. Fredersen, locked, solidified, as if Sovann was looking at a sculpture.

He called to Fredersen again, but he did not answer. Nothing about Fredersen moved. The mightiest man in all Metropolis stood inert.

As if feeling a sort of guilt at breaching the stipulation that he not talk to Jurgen Fredersen, he went to see the other parts of the Tower. He had visited three levels of Fredersen's employees, the Brain-Pan of the Tower, his inner circle all with their fancy suits and slicked hair, all at their desks or checking the ticker tape, and all of them in a stasis of absolute petrification. None of them exhibited any movements. All of the other people that he saw on the three levels he visited were rigid, as if snapped into an immovable photograph. The ticker tape was not forthcoming as it usually was, and neither were the stock prices from the other cities of the world—London, Peking, Tokio. All business, from Sovann's inspection, had come to a standstill.

"Hello?" he constantly tried. There was no response from the silent humans, unmoving, encased as if in amber. But there was nothing to hinder their movement.

They were still flesh and blood, there were pulses, and he also confirmed that they were breathing, yet they were all absolutely stock still, hardened into their positions. He saw someone communicating through televideophone, but the person on the screen was also rigid, immobile. The screen was still activated, the call was still in progress, but the other person on the line was frozen mid-sentence.

"What is going on here?" Sovann lamented now, loudly. He raised his voice further. Still, no response from these immotile beings. Sovann embraced himself as he went back to the night watchman's living quarters above.

Not a thing was stirring in Metropolis. The whole sprawling megalopolis, the city that was the last word for cities, was dormant, stuck in time.

He waited for the ten hour shift whistle that traveled through the city, ear-splitting as always. This would be a major clue, if the whistle would blast through the city as it usually did. He waited for twenty-one hours and didn't hear the regular siren to the workers.

Now shaking to the core, he took a chance and wandered the streets of the city, not before arming himself with a hand-sized revolver. Everywhere he went, people were caught and frozen in the middle of something, whether walking, looking into a shop window, or strolling about. All of them looked to be doing activity expected during the time he kept encountering on all timepieces: 3:17 a.m.

Sovann saw a policeman chasing a suspect, their action fossilized in air. He saw the masses of the workers, their heads turned to the ground, one foot above the ground to form a step, one on the ground, all paralyzed, all immovable. He saw people in cars, the motions of driving all at an abrupt stop, all of them as still as mannequins in various states of still life. He pinched them, prodded them, sometimes even knocking them to the ground. They all remained stock static in their positions in spite of all he did to them.

Donning on his graviton boots, Sovann wore these as he walked the sides of Metropolis's buildings, looking into every window. He climbed up buildings sideways, walked up walls and skyscrapers edgewise, sidewise, laterally, horizontally, a lone figure exploring the city. Walking on ceilings, he searched for company, looked to see if anyone was active. He entered private apartments and luxurious tenements. At each peek into the private lives of the citizens, he saw that they were all stationary in what looked like theatrical poses. Yet these poses, normally mundane, took on an altogether different meaning now, and this signified alarm for him and encompassing loneliness.

The terror of it started to eat away at him, though he swore that he wouldn't let it. How was it that he, of all millions of dwellers of Metropolis, was the only person able to move about? He wondered at how this was even possible. Evidently, something happened to him only or to the entire denizens of Metropolis at 3:17 in the morning. Usually he was tending to his responsibilities at that time, so why did he wake slightly after dawn?

✛✛✛

All of Metropolis was his.

The generators that the Master Builders of Metropolis had installed had activated. There was electricity available at night so Sovann wasn't plunged in inky darkness as he expected. The power that the massive generators supplied was sufficient, emitting a soft glow rather than Metropolis's regular glaring incandescence.

He had taken Jurgen Fredersen's clothing and the finest things Metropolis had to offer. Suddenly, he no longer ate like a pauper—expensive and indulgent food was available to him in the affluent areas. His company was birdsong and breezes. His radio at the apex of the Tower was constantly on, a dead drone of monotone noise. He danced with the standstill people at Frothland, dancing to silence and his inner music. Entering the G-Bank of Metropolis, he procured an ample amount of bank notes from there, money that had no meaning now. The rare plants of the Eternal Gardens were his, along with the most expensive paintings from the museums, which he hung with admiration in his now well-stocked quarters at the Tower.

Also accompanying him were the prohibited books from the Library of the Sons. Sovann had walked past the incapacitated guards, each one a living statue frozen possibly forever in a Metropolis moment. He took the books he wanted and read them, rare volumes formerly reserved for the Sons, edifying himself and alleviating the loneliness that now beset him. The tales of adventure sustained him, brought him through the sureality of his plight, the pages worth more than mined gold to him.

He still avoided visiting the Workers' City and its human cattle, instead opting to take a car to the outskirts of Metropolis to see if the surrounding areas were also in deadlock. While the citizens were immotile in their cars, he found that all he had to do was turn the ignition and in some cases a car would start.

Driving to the outside took some hours since traffic was in an expected immovable gridlock. Oftentimes, he was completely barricaded by cars, the drivers inside each car not twitching a muscle. He saw that the surrounding areas of the city were also in the same exact state as the city.

Sovann had to know if this was all just him, that he was the only person affected, or the other possibility, that everyone besides him were affected at 3:17 a.m. that enigmatic night.

Dining in the most exclusive and stuffiest of clubs, wearing the costliest tie clips to secure his ties, he started to talk to himself. Pretending to have company, he would act the part of someone dining with him, which Sovann later thought to be slightly morbid when he returned to his home at the Tower.

All of Metropolis was his.

✠✠✠

Faced horizontally and walking down the side of the elevator shaft into the Workers' City, graviton allowing him to bypass the bleak elevators to below, he shivered. Having searched the millions of people of Metropolis for an intelligible soul, the Workers' City was the last hope of finding someone who could talk. Perhaps there was something in the depths of the underground that could explain what has happened to the city.

There the workers were, the mole-people, many in front of the grand machine locally known for its penchant to sometimes kill its workers by accident. These workers, the hands who built Metropolis, were geometrically arrayed, their movements in the pause of clockwork. In the Machine District, he viewed the Heart Machine, the main power source to the entire city, and saw the Geyser Machine. He encountered the generators, the hum pervading the area around them with steam emitting in great billows, along with the Human Clocks whose operators' misery had no bounds.

Having talked to the workers, their frowns deadlocked and their looks of exhaustion at dead stop on their faces, Sovann had encountered no one who could converse. He checked their pulses and they were alive, yet were rigid statues like the aboveground people. The children of the city all looked to be malnourished and were in grimy, ragged smocks, immobilized and barefoot. The women of the city all wore the same drab skirts and blouses, as all the hunched workers wore the blue denim from head to foot and those ever-present caps stating their worker digits and their names.

Having searched the entire Workers' City, he went further below, to the Metropolis Catacombs that he had read about. The Catacombs were two thousand years old, Stygian, foreboding. He brought candles with him, lighting the way around human skulls in recesses, bones from various parts of the human anatomical structure, and rocky, unsmooth caves. As Sovann called, his voice reverberated through the chambers, echoing back on him. He kept calling, standing still to hear if anyone had made a sound. There was no sound besides that of steady water trickling through the roofs of the catacombs.

He returned to the Workers' City, having had a systematic look to see if anyone was in the caverns. He again saw the people who were under the absolute thumb of the Master, Jurgen Fredersen. He saw how the Upper Ten Thousand kept those below in check by keeping them too tired to be able to mount any sort of action against their Master above. At least now they could not hear the siren every ten hours to their brutal work shifts. Perhaps it was good that all of the Workers' City was inert. Walking the walls of the vertical elevator tunnel back to the aboveground, he thought at least they were spared their suffering due to the total inertia he had witnessed since that fateful time of 3:17 a.m.

✝✝✝

Sovann searched the Library of the Sons for answers. Mostly, he had kept books from there to keep him company as he read by the soft nighttime glow that the subterranean generators provided.

If it was only about him, that he was stuck in time, then he had to find a way to get back into the natural flow. If it was all of the people of Metropolis besides himself that were inanimate, then it would go to reason that the whole world would also be in the same state of dormancy since no one from the other cities and countries of the globe had arrived to Metropolis to start investigating the cause.

He had felt that it had to be the former, that it was only him welded to a pinpoint in time, able to move about, stuck within an infinite minute.

And he pondered infinity—what was infinity like? Would he live to infinity as well? If he was alone, then what use would never dying be? Already the loneliness was beginning to be unbearable.

He still searched Metropolis for Thandiwe and had not found her. Since that first night of being in Metropolis, the memory of who he had met had haunted him. He still held up hope. If only she could see him now, in a dangerous position at the very summit of the entire city, on top of the New Tower of Babel. If only she could see that he was clothed resplendently as a Fredersen.

Returning to his former rundown tenement, he searched for her calling card again, and it was nowhere to be found.

Many were his diversions to deflect his alarming predicament. Aside from searching in the Library of the Sons for any clues to the matter, he walked boots above head on the opalescent arched ceiling of the Eternal Gardens, his pair of graviton boots walking the concave glass. Marveling at his unfettered freedom, he would stare down into the lush recreation grounds built for the Sons and marvel at what he now owned. For him, it now seemed as if he was the mightiest man in Metropolis, that he had become Jurgen Fredersen.

Though he resisted, many times he saw gin being made in the bathtubs of hotels and illicit, sparkling green absinthe in the bars of Yoshiwara and the Club of the Sons. There was temptation to slake his thirst to forget his loneliness and drench himself away in this form of escape. Yet he was wise enough to keep his defenses.

He wandered the opium dens of another level of Metropolis, located in the back-alleys, sorely tempted to dissolve himself in an opium haze, but reasoned that he needed to be in complete control of his wits if he was to figure out what he was facing.

Sovann saw parties frozen in place, dreamlike sights of bobbed hair, strings of pearls, champagne, cigarette holders, dancers frozen in the Charleston, people waist-deep and unmoving in champagne fountains. He loved to see spats on shiny shoes as silent jazz floated imaginary through the air.

He visited the gangsters running the underground, for they were evidently the brotherhood behind the flow of alcohol into Metropolis. He played with their faces and knocked them to the ground. He took their tommy guns and replaced the bullets with pellets or whipped cream. He took what looked to be the head of a gangster unit and placed his rigid body in one of the prisons of the police wards, locking and throwing the key into a fountain on the other side of the city.

It was nearing a month as he returned to his abode, feeling on top of the world, the Master of all he surveyed, yet simultaneously feeling to be in the deepest of anguish. It was a disturbing state to be in.

And the radio he kept on with hope continued with its static.

✠✠✠

While Sovann knew that the outer limits of the city were all in the same state, he considered going back to his former life in the village. He only thought of going since perhaps it was a form of going back home, even if those he knew would be flash comatose in place. Later, he found that he couldn't give up his new life, that to drive all the way back would be going away from the center of the world. Sovann felt that the answer was somewhere in Metropolis.

It was now that he was given to states of absinthe-fueled dreams. It was the absinthe from the Club of the Sons, locked behind museum quality glass. What at first became a small indulgence soon became a daily consuming. He was careful not to walk with the gravity-inducing boots while in his drunken fugues for a part of him still wanted to correct the riveted state of his city.

It was while Sovann had combined water with absinthe, forming a cloudy louche in a pontarlier glass, that he heard the motor above.

His boots securing him from the occasionally strong and dangerous gusts of the very height of the New Tower of Babel, he felt that perhaps the mechanical sound was a figment of his imagination, perhaps a symptom of the wormwood in his green liquid.

It was then that he saw the zeppelin emerge from the fringed lining of clouds, hovering majestically, heading to his position on top of the Tower.

Blinking his eyes at the sight, he tossed off his gas mask and screamed his very being toward the airship. Waving his hands in the air and generating all the movement he could, the zeppelin continued on its steady course toward where Sovann was perched.

Closer the zeppelin came to the Tower, Sovann's heart rate increasing as it started to manifest diligently nearer.

It couldn't possibly land on the New Tower of Babel as its top surface size wasn't ample for landing that enormous of a ship.

Now slightly above the Tower, Sovann cupped his hands and yelled, projecting his voice, his lungs, to the compartment holding the controllers guiding the ship.

He saw puzzled faces in the windows, but they were moving. This was the first time Sovann had seen the movements of humans in more than a month.

A door opened in the ship, hands stirring as a rope ladder was extended to where Sovann was. A man and two women were looking curiously at him. Sovann was so eager for human contact that he disregarded any hesitations in entering.

Hastily, he climbed the ladder, his boots still on him, leaving the gas mask behind. They threw out their hands as he neared the entrance to their posh cabin, helping him in the rest of the way.

The hatch closed and he viewed four people, all of whom stared the same mutual stare that he gave them.

☩☩☩

"Are you one of the Sons of the City?" was the first question posed to him, this time by what looked to be an elderly lady of golden years.

Waving his hands in the air...

"I am not, I'm just arrayed that way," he said, explaining his entire story up until they had found him as the airship flew above Metropolis.

"What has happened to Metropolis?" asked Sovann.

A gentleman with pomaded flaxen hair responded that it was not only Metropolis, it was the whole world.

"As far as we know," he said, authoritatively, "it's not just Metropolis. It's the entire earth. If you will notice, we have the 3:17 a.m. hands locked on our clocks as well. Something originated from Metropolis at that time to paralyze the entire globe."

"Indeed," added a young vamp type with shiny red lipstick. She held a vast feather in one hand, sweeping it around her face, fanning it and moving it in the area around her. "We were in one of the highest strata of the earth for weeks, enjoying our little party here on this ship. It was not until we came to normal strata did we realize that Metropolis and the rest of the world are unconscious."

Sovann still felt that he was in the effects of his dalliance with the Sons' absinthe.

"Sit here," said the man with the flaxen hair as he drew up an ornately upholstered chair for Sovann.

"That's a mighty story you have given us, working your way from a lantern bearer to the night watchman of the New Tower," he commented. "What's next?" he added in a rhetorical, jolly way, cerulean eyes acknowledging to the rest of his party.

"Finding out the cause of all of this," Sovann replied as a middle-aged and bearded pilot turned his head and nodded in his direction for the first time.

"We have been traveling the world since, and everywhere, everyone is in the same state. Mazagan, Rio, Trondhjem, Lakhnau, Montreal, Nanking, Constantinople. It's the same everywhere. The world has stopped at 3:17 a.m.," said the pilot. "We're the only ones moving. It is only now that we come back to Metropolis to search for the cause," he added.

"Are you all from Metropolis?" inquired Sovann.

"We are," said the vamp, looking deeply into her hand mirror.

"Why do you think that we are the only people on earth who are able to move?" asked Sovann.

"That is what we are determined to find out, as determined as you were in your searches through Metropolis," said the blond fellow.

"There has to be some reason. This can't be an accident," suggested Sovann.

"We've been speculating and ruminating on it," said the young woman, looking only at her reflection in the glass, "but you see, we are as much in the dark about it as you. We also have a feeling that the effect rippled outward from Metropolis as the central point, encircling the ends of the planet. For some reason, we, high above in the thermosphere, were spared, like you."

"Professor Saavedra here has invented the first airship to fly through the earth's thermosphere," said the younger man.

"It's the bee's knees," said the vamp.

"Well, we know your name. My name's Irma," said the elegantly clad elderly female. She extended her hand.

Sovann held it nonchalantly and lightly kissed it as a sign of greeting.

"Well, if you are not one of the Sons of Metropolis, you do act like one," Irma blushed.

"Mine's Margaret, but you can call me Zellde," replied the mirror-obsessed young woman.

"And mine's Billy," said the dapper fellow. "I'm an archaeologist who at the moment is specializing in parties and touring around with Professor Saavedra here. The Professor, as you can gather, is a scientist of aeronautics and aerodynamics."

Saavedra gave a modest nod to what Billy stated.

"We were all alone in the world, but now, less alone. For you, I hope your loneliness will clear," mused Irma.

He had not told them about Thandiwe.

"At least that bastard Jurgen Fredersen is unable to touch that infernal blue plate that calls all the workers," said Zellde. "We really should bring him down to the depths of the Workers' City. In fact, let's put him in front of that goddamn Moloch machine and see how he likes it."

The others in the plush cabin all remained neutral.

"Foremost on our minds is to search Metropolis, though we know you've come to a standstill, pun intended," said Billy. "Professor Saavedra here has hypothesized that we were spared because what emitted from Metropolis was emitted into a curved pattern that wrapped around the earth. These fields grew forth in a curved V-pattern, with Metropolis being at the bottom point of the V. Those of us within the V-shape were spared, which includes this ship and you on your Tower."

"This is the working hypothesis of the Professor's at the moment, and he is rarely wrong," added Zellde.

Sovann still thought that it could possibly be a time issue rather than a physics issue, that there was room for something to the effect that had shattered the regular workings of time.

Zellde proceeded to light up a cigarette after putting aside her ever-present mirror. She placed the cigarette into an ivory holder and looked at Sovann with relish.

"By the way, you're a real sheikh, mister," she said to Sovann. "If we were not in this circumstance," her eyebrows lifting, "well, you know what I mean. But I'm here on a scientific expedition now, as it is. I must be the last 'flapper' remaining in the world."

"You're very forward, Miss Zellde," was all Sovann could say.

"You're damn right I am. Now, sheikh, let's put all of our heads together to get us out of this conundrum?"

"I do remember you saying that the world should remain this way," recalled Billy, looking at Zellde.

"Exactly. Why keep the misery going? Humans still have a long way to go. Not including us, excluding us, you know. We're more advanced than warfare and nationhood. To think, for us to be known as 'that planet' on the edge of this galaxy, the boondocks of the galaxy, really, still trying to find our way to become cohesive. It boggles the mind. Sometimes I feel as if I've waken into an intolerant dimension in the mornings. Just to think of the world wars."

She sighed as she looked at the rest of the cabin through the cobalt hued smoke permeating the air from her holder.

"Well, at least there are parties. I absolutely live for parties, and I suppose that is the redeeming grace of today's society. We all live for parties."

"I suppose that is correct," said Sovann.

"I absolutely adore the way you're raiding Metropolis while it's in this state. We should all do the same, at least, before we solve this complex dilemma. Have some fun! When are we going to have another chance like this, ever?"

As usual, her cabin mates took in Zellde's meditations with amusement and reflection.

"I want to see everything. The Workers' City, the Catacombs, the Eternal Gardens, the Club of the Sons, Frothland, Seitenschiene, Akbar, everything that Metropolis has to offer," enthused Zellde.

"Since us five, Sovann, are the only unfrozen in time people," said Billy, "why not make it worth our while, indulging in everything the city contains? I know you will agree. You deserve it most of all, after what has happened with the water infections in your village. But never you mind that now."

The night watchman agreed as well. He felt far less lonely and less alarmed now that he had company to talk with and to uncover the source of the mystery.

"You know I agree to it. And how!" said Zellde.

Irma nodded her head, a pleasant smile on her matronly face.

Professor Saavedra gave the thumbs up from his piloting chair.

Billy talked briefly with the Professor and came back to the cabin.

"The Professor will be looking for an urtext that explains the workings and beginnings of the building of Metropolis, to be sure, for some insights as to the situation. Perhaps an urtext or something similar can be found in the Library of the Sons."

They continued on their aerial journey of Metropolis, seeing it from the windows of the traveling cabin attached to the zeppelin, seeing the city as if it were a remarkable toy, the city of multitudes of stratoscrapers and bewildering multilevels of urban sprawl.

The Professor guided the ship to where the other flying machines and airplanes were suspended in the air. All five of them could see the immobile pilots in their concentration and the passengers that were in catatonic states, some also looking down onto Metropolis, all wonderstruck as indicated by their fixed features. The Professor guided the ship as close as possible to these planes and aircraft that were stationary in the air. To Sovann, it felt entirely uncanny to be seeing this, while the other four took a scientific interest in it, observing all that they could with their data gathering propensities.

After passing by two more of the suspended in the air biplanes and other machines of aerial conveyance, they felt that they had enough of viewing Metropolis from above, so Professor Saavedra proceeded to fly the airship to the surrounding areas of the city limits, confirming for Sovann that only they, the five of them, were mobile of all the people.

Sovann was glad about the new friends and human interaction after feeling to be the loneliest person in existence.

✠✠✠

They had found the Fredersen Airport of Metropolis and had landed lightly on a clear airstrip.

This was what Zellde, Billy, and Irma were waiting for: to raid Metropolis just as Sovann had done.

Sovann went along as they explored the city, the cars stopped, the trains halted, everything locked as if in a snapshot.

First, they visited taverns, lodges, gentlemen's clubs, and exclusive indoor golf clubs located on uppermost floors of the towers of the Upper Ten Thousand. They freely took the Metropolis bank notes from the gentry's pockets, with Zellde taking strings of pearls from the rooted to the spot Daughters of Metropolis. Zellde soon had the finest jewelry, and it pleased her as she looked into her hand mirror. Zellde screamed in delight as she unburdened the Metropolitan elite with discoveries here and there of the world's rarest gemstones, finding benitoite, alexandrite, taaffeite, red beryl, and the rarest mineral of all, painite. She now owned these flashy treasures with no intention of giving them back.

In contrast, Irma wasn't much a jewelry fanatic, but was very much obsessed by the millinery of high society Metropolitans. Within just three hours of touring the best of the best Daughters' Clubs, she had a collection of hats befitting royalty. She amassed hats made of the rarest materials, and even a hat fabricated entirely from spider silk, knowing that spider silk is five times as strong as steel.

Professor Saavedra's riches were the rare tomes, books, incunabula, and scrolls housed in the Library of the Sons. He immediately began to work, saying to his party, now including Sovann, a pithy witticism: "Most things in life are impermanent. Very few things in life are permanent and most things only tarry for a while, and then are gone. What is permanent is literature and art. These are the two constants guaranteed to be non-ephemeral."

Irma added, "Yes, Professor, things in life come and go, a constant state of flux, a revolving door of people and situations. Happiness, when found, must be grabbed and enjoyed. Even these hats I have collected I know to not last forever. But art and literature are the only things that are not washed away by the tide of time like sand castles facing ocean tides."

Sovann thought this to be absolutely accurate. The stories told in books and the images of art stay eternally while it seems that everything else in life can be fleeting.

They visited the G-Bank and took bars of gold and paper notes, also taking interesting contents from safety deposit boxes. The car they had was almost to the brim with all of their new belongings.

The pair of graviton boots were lent to Billy, who walked sideways and upside down through Seitenschiene, a Johnny-jumper club known for its bohemian balls. Walking on its walls and on the ceiling gave him a fine view of the crowded night spot. He took fine watches and drank the contents of the glasses of the revelers, taking care to not knock anyone over as the place was filled to the brim.

Irma was curious in visiting the Metropolis Cathedral, a Gothic structure lending an incongruous beauty next to the behemoth-sized architectural masterpieces of the city. Telling Zellde of the Seven Deadly Sins statues of marble in the cathedral, she had immediately regretted it because Zellde wanted to enact all of them while all of Metropolis was theirs.

"Let's see. I've already got pride in full force," itemized Zellde. "Greed we've certainly nailed since we've taken from the G-Bank and the museums. Metropolis's aboveground embodies greed, doesn't it? Lust, well, let me be on the level: I've just met you, Sovann, and think that perhaps, well, you know.

Now as for gluttony, I say we dine in Metropolis's snobbiest restaurant tonight: Haus 496. Steaks, white pearl caviar, spiced saffron cakes, truffles, the world's most luxurious fare, all for us to glut upon."

The Professor was still searching for some information that would lend to the unraveling of the petrified state of the city and the globe, but consented to dine with them at Haus 496 in the elegant Holbein Room. They had a toast as Zellde climbed onto the table, walking between their dishes, clearly affected by the consumption of champagne with edible gold. Truly enjoying themselves, they burst into song at times and felt a sense of mirth, despite the world's quiet state. The Professor, Billy, and Sovann lit the most expensive cigars, with Zellde partaking along, her cigar totteringly close to falling to the ground.

"As to wrath, as I've told you before, I think wrath is all horsefeathers. Maybe we can do a simulated form of wrath, but we can choose to move to sloth, which I find abhorrent. I always like to be productive."

They had feasted as they looked from the decorated crystal windows, ornate, semiprecious gems glinting from the casements. Earlier they had moved aside the static diners at their table and partook of the most extravagant food available at the restaurant that was reserved for the Sons and the Fathers of Metropolis.

"Zellde, I believe you have a good notion here: we may be the only people left in the world that are mobile, and you have found a way to stave off melancholy. We should all have your joie de vivre, the spirit of life."

"I'm, well, I'm a bit zozzled at the moment, to state the obvious, Professor," she remarked as she almost fell to the floor, then resuming her bearing on the table, standing as if on some sort of make-believe pedestal. "I've been a Metropolitan for eons. I'll go back to being a staid 'Mrs. Grundy' when we get Metropolis back on its feet. Of that, I have no doubt."

They all had partaken of the most sumptuous feast of their lives.

"As to envy," said Professor Saavedra, "what is there left to envy? We have everything. All I envy, really, is those who have found love. What do you envy, Irma?"

"I'm so full right now I could burst!" Irma exclaimed as she looked through the fortified crystal windows to revel in the elevated region the restaurant was at in the sky. She contemplated the flying machines suspended in air over the city, so close to Haus 496, stagnant since they were caught in the paralysis area of Saavedra's proposed V-shape fields.

"What do I envy? I envy those who never feel lonely. Even though I have you as friends, still, I'm sure you can agree that sometimes loneliness seeps in.

That's what I envy. Now your turn, Zellde. Time to envy."

Still standing shakily on the table where they were dining, she didn't take long to express what she envied.

"You may think this bushwa, but I envy those who have children. Someday I want my own."

"Oh, tell it to Sweeney, Zellde," ventured Irma, not believing.

"Really," Zellde said, her inebriated eyes suddenly taking a faraway look, some gravitas added. "That's what I envy."

There was silence for a moment as they pondered this.

"And now your turn, Billy. What do you envy?" asked Irma.

Billy was flush full of wine, having had a bit too much of it, captivated at the edible platinum within. His face had a ruddy and distorted cast to it, the ruddiness mingling with the glorious sunset's light that began to coat the immovable city in a paradisiacal sandy glow.

"Envy, what I envy," he cogitated. "We've taken the spoils of Metropolis, so there's nothing lacking for materialism. Look at us, all gussied up in the finest threads. When you mentioned envy, something immediately came to mind. I suppose we envy people who are unequivocally happy. And what brings happiness? Happiness cannot be bought. It's not purchased in the Club of the Sons or in any of the fancy shops of Metropolis. What brings happiness is a sense of belonging, of the approbation of other people. Therefore, in this instance, I'd have to say I envy not having the company of other people at the moment. Which is to not denigrate the company I have at present, I adore all of you. So yes, that's my answer."

They all applauded as they continued with slaking gluttony.

"As you can see," said the Professor, "no one has yet mentioned anything material. The responses to this deadly sin of envy only brought forth the immaterial. I would also like to say that in our present circumstance, I envy those who have ever gotten married. I've been unswerving in my commitment to knowledge and the process of invention that I have had no time for a personal life."

"Well, I said I wanted children, but I never said that I wanted a wedding ring on. Who wants a handcuff on their ring finger?"

"To each their own, my dear, to each their own," said the Professor.

All now turned to Sovann, who had such a distant look to his expression.

"I envy wherever Thandiwe is at the moment," he whispered audibly.

✝✝✝

They had adjourned to the night watchman's quarters at the New Tower of Babel. It had started to thunderstorm in the city, lightning flashing to light up the immensely dark sky, startling booms rumbling through the city that felt preternatural, seeming to shake the Tower's glass windows as if with hands. Metropolis was still being powered by the generators under the city, the soft glow continuing through the walls of rain.

Sovann had told them all about Thandiwe, how he had met her for one night, only to have her lost within the fifty-five million inhabitants of the city.

"We know without doubt that she is comatose like everyone else and somewhere in the city. But, please do not be offended by this, Sovann: why would you want to be with someone from Metropolis's night? Those kinds can never be tied down," said Irma, her eyes sharp from beneath her spider silk hat.

"I felt a spark I'd never felt before. Sometimes you just feel it. What the villagers back home had told me was absolutely correct, it would happen when I wasn't searching for it."

"Sovann," said the Professor. "This is Metropolis. It's all new to you. Though it is Metropolis, I can concur partly with Irma's sentiment about the nighttime denizens here, but these are just generalizations, and sweeping generalizations are usually unfair. We don't know since we weren't there to experience it. Only you know the situation best."

"I was searching the city, half in fear of finding her and what my reaction would be to her being stationary in time. I just want to know where she is, that's all, and who's holding Thandiwe now."

"Say, mister, you've got it real deep, don't you? You're really stuck on her, aren't you?" emitted Zellde, her head between her hands, her arms balanced on a table made of chased silver and dichroic glass. Sovann's quarters had all the best of Metropolis, including several original Van Goghs and the Leonardo da Vinci painting of Ginevra de' Benci as well. Zellde regretted enacting the seven deadly sins because it had interrupted their blissful escapades through Metropolis. She immediately distracted herself with looking into her new mirror as was her wont, a Roman Empire-era hand mirror in fine condition from one of Metropolis's history museums.

The thunder roared as they looked at the city around them.

After a third remarkable boom of thunder that vibrated the Tower, they were plunged into darkness.

The lights that illuminated the evening, the soft glow that the generators had produced for the entire city, had ceased to function.

Irma immediately held herself in a tight embrace.

His arms waving through the darkness, Billy was able to find a chair only when flashes of lightning revealed the arrangement of the quarters.

...looking into her new hand mirror...

"Oh, this is the berries," said Zellde with sarcasm. "Doggone it, now how do we save Metropolis?"

✝✝✝

They waited through the rolling, roaring night until morning, Sovann lighting the candles he had available in the quarters. It had drawn cold as the night progressed, the adventurers shivering, their teeth chattering.

For the first time, Sovann felt fear in Metropolis. The dark raging above had sent more than its share of shivers to the crew as they huddled together all night in the candlelight. They were mostly soundless as the thunder rolled cacophonously, the waves of sound seeming to shake the very foundations of the Tower, threatening to topple where they were at their grand height.

It was with a sense of hope and relief that dawn lit another glorious morning on the city, imbuing the unstuck party. Once they determined that the skies had calmed, they took the elevator and exited to see the people of Metropolis soaking wet, startlingly joyous expressions on their faces, oblivious to their drenching.

The plan was to get back to the airstrip to their ship, which had built-in generators powered on Saavedra's patented energy source. The Professor wanted to bring Sovann's radio and have it function within the airship.

All of Metropolis remained at a standstill, and all of Metropolis was soaked in the renewed sun.

"Well, the party's not quite over. We can still acquire what we think we want before getting back onto our ship," said Irma.

They were all silent to her remark.

Their loneliness was starting to encroach upon them. Before they had descended from the Tower, Irma and Billy were making paper airplanes of the money they had acquired from Metropolis's G-Bank. They were launching these through a window that the Professor had managed to open for fresh air.

Irma had a pensive and melancholic expression as she wistfully tossed the airplanes on their flight.

She whispered quietly, audible only to herself.

"What's that you say, Irma?" asked the Professor politely, his emotions contained.

This startled Irma from her reverie.

"What use is money when there is no one around," she replied, barely hearable, but still her words traveled through the night watchman's quarters.

"Yes. Yes, indeed," was the Professor's response, and he sauntered up beside the two, folding the Metropolis tender from the floor into intricate aerodynamic designs and joining them in launching them from the Tower window.

Sovann could only stare, still shaken, as could Zellde find herself to also only stare. All of their newfound riches, and yet they were just things now, mere things.

They took nothing with them from the Tower besides what they were wearing, leaving behind all of what they amassed from the city.

Finding a shop that had the vastest collection of radios, the Professor had found a radio that was lightweight, portable, efficient on energy, and covered the breadth of all bands for reception.

After walking by the silent Workers' Whistle, its structure towering in itself, the Professor's ship was found where they had placed it, the ship still intact. They went back to the city, acquiring any food they could find, whether it be from a mendicant's or a Son's meal, and launched into the stratosphere. Once in the air above Metropolis, they felt more of a sense of control and safety as the electricity hummed through the cabin. They hovered for a bit, wondering where they could possibly go since the entire world was catatonic.

The radio plugged in, all they heard was static, humming through the evening as they slept while the Professor stood at the console, staring, thinking, reflecting.

The skies were clear that night and without tempest. They slept soundly as the Professor agreed to take watch through the night.

Sovann slept nearest to the radio, his graviton boots on for practicality, while Zellde looked crestfallen as she looked at a lightless Metropolis from the airship, undiscernible in the night, almost as if the city had never existed. Eventually she had taken to a peaceful rest, while Irma still had a hypnotized look, as if distancing herself from reality. Billy had a look of alarm on his face, remembering the good times they just had and reflecting on the powerless generators that daubed a becalmed glow only twelve hours before.

✝✝✝

"Professor? Professor!"

He had woken to the sound of Irma's voice, in a loud panic.

"It's the Professor!" she screamed. "He's not moving!"

The morning light streamed into the cabin, and Sovann had rubbed his eyes.

There was Billy, immediately looking to see if what Irma said was true. He shook the Professor, even slapped him, but the Professor was stock-still, rigid, as inflexible as all of the citizens of Metropolis in the pilot's chair, his hands rigid in place near the controls.

"Zellde, come here and help us," implored Billy, barely containing his stressed voice.

There was no response.

"Zellde!" Billy repeated, looking to where she was. "Zell—"

"Oh my stars," whispered Irma.

Zellde was as frozen as the rest, seeming to be asleep, but as motionless as a film still.

Billy confirmed the pulses of both and proceeded to move the Professor gently to the co-pilot's seat. Another tempest was headed their way from looking at the horizon, and Billy wanted to get the airship to a safer distance.

Irma had fallen to the floor, her hands on her mouth, eyes full.

"Not the Professor and Zellde," her voice trailing to inaudibility.

"I can't fathom why, Irma, why we three are unaffected? What's in store for us now?" bellowed Billy as he piloted the ship to a higher altitude above the clouds to avoid the snares of another threatening tempest, the whole ship at such a sharp incline that everything in the cabin was sliding, Irma and Sovann holding on to prevent their own slipping.

"The Professor has always been right," said Irma, recalling the V-shape hypothesis of paralyzing rays emitted from a source in Metropolis.

"Is it someone? Something? What could be causing this? We're the only three people left in the world now," the flaxen haired man said.

"And what if I'm the only person left in the world?" screamed Irma, frightening Billy and Sovann.

"What if all of us remaining are put in the same state? There will be no one left in all the world. Then the world will just fade away," their current pilot said.

"We can't give way to panic and hopelessness right now. Come on, Irma, have cheer, for our sake. We need to put our heads together."

These words from Billy caused Irma to plant herself into a state of placid suspension after her raving. Diagonal in Billy's flight, she emerged after a while back into their situation, her scientific, rational, unemotional mind taking over, the left hemisphere of her mind conquering.

Irma ventured to speak after a period of silence once the ship stabilized.

"Yes, indeed, Billy. You have piloted us to a safer height and we'll begin to form new hypotheses. I already have some in mind."

"So do I," replied Billy.

Irma moved to a section of the cabin that held all of Professor Saavedra's books, treatises, engineering schematics, and handwritten journal entries.

Before reaching the cabin, she turned the radio's volume up louder so she could hear it better, though still leaving room to hear her cabin mates. If anyone could bring Irma to her operable, efficient state, it was Billy.

Sovann was amazed at the resiliency of the two, as if they had both slipped into a mode of thinking that was detached, as if they had suddenly become calculators computing for Mersenne primes or a flight window to the inner planets of the system.

"Is there anything I can do?" asked Sovann, feeling a bit out of place, as if they had ignored him.

"Indeed, Sovann, I was just going to mention. Can you draw? I need you to create some etchings. This will come as a bit of a shock to you, but the Professor discovered it and confided it only amongst Zellde, me, and Billy, having located a dusty tome after breaking the glass casement to get to it in the Library of the Sons.

"There is an underground castle beneath the Catacombs of Metropolis."

Sovann thought he had known the entire breadth and width of the city during his solo wanderings before the zeppelin arrived. His mouth was agape as he looked to both of them, who returned serious looks to him.

"And while I decipher the Professor's Gordian hand script, I will describe to you the way we can get there while Billy pilots the ship. We'll get through this.

"For now, Billy, continue into the deepest layer of the thermosphere, perhaps we'll be more shielded against these unknown fields that have affected the Professor, Zellde, and the rest of the world. It's up to us three to save it all now."

"All things thrive at the triplex," said Billy as he took the ship up.

✛✛✛

Sovann still felt that it could possibly be him who remained stuck in the infinite loop of a minute, a 3:17 a.m. that stretched on boundlessly. All of these people from the sky, their situation, what they did, could all have been entirely of his imagining.

He learned that the castle beneath the Catacombs was built by Jurgen Fredersen in the days before Metropolis was built, but then he was challenged to vaster plans as he dreamt of Metropolis and its realization. The castle was still there, neglected all these years, formerly Jurgen's private sanctuary. Irma remarked that it was the only place in Metropolis that none of their party had searched.

Taking the risk of becoming petrified, the three landed at the airstrip and proceeded to follow Sovann's map to where the castle was most likely located.

Running in a panic since they felt they were in the solidification zone, they constantly checked each other to see that they were all still moving. It was during their rush through the city, dodging the eerie stock-still figures, that Sovann found Thandiwe at last.

Thandiwe was in the arms of a man Sovann didn't recognize, the two kissing closely, locked in a full embrace.

"Thandiwe. It can't be," Sovann said as he slowed his movement to see Thandiwe's face, authenticating it to be the woman he had fallen for his first evening in the city.

"Sovann, we have to keep moving! We're ever so sorry, however we must save this city and our friends! You can talk to Thandiwe if we restore Metropolis!" panted Billy, sweat in rivulets cascading from his forehead.

Sovann tried to hold the inner flood welling up within, but had to be as resilient as Irma and Billy, task ahead of them, focused.

Pulling on one of the graviton boots on his right leg, Billy handed the other one to Sovann, who put it on his left leg. In between them they held Irma as they descended horizontally into the vertical shaft that led to the Workers' City. They located the Catacombs, Billy using artificial illumination powered by the reserve energy from the airship. Their feet crunching on skeletons, they followed the Professor's descriptions and navigated a complex network of tunnels, zigzagging, meandering, snaking.

Having nearly lost their way a few times after running down tunnels manufactured as decoys, they at last found Jurgen Fredersen's castle.

It was made entirely of amethyst, its turrets sparkling in the gloom. The moat held boulders of glinting gold and silver rather than water, and the drawbridge was ready, welcoming.

Catching their breaths, they were overwhelmed at the absolute beauty of the hidden fortress. The bridge they were treading on was also of pure amethyst, and it all looked so brittle that they wondered if they should be taking more caution.

They entered the main keep, and heard sound and saw candlelight from a drawing room within. Entering the room, Billy immediately took cover as a woman in a lab coat aimed at him and pulled a trigger. The wickedly tinted ray barely missed him, but it had hit someone unknown to them who was closing in on Billy. The minion was immediately made static, as unmoving as everyone else affected.

Irma had hidden beneath an amethyst counter while Sovann had rushed up to the woman, leaping, pinning her down and throwing the ray gun to Billy, who seized it and gave it to Irma. Irma pointed it at the woman and was ready should anyone else enter the drawing room.

The woman struggled under the grip of both men as Irma placed her boot on her forehead.

"Now, tell us what is the meaning of this. What have you done to the world?"

Her struggles to no avail, she immediately calmed, then started to weep, her sobs wracking her. The party did not release their grip, impeding her to the floor. Held in place, she looked at the formulae, the imaginary unit functions, and the non-Euclidean object properties that she had etched onto the amethyst walls, lustrous from the radiance of dozens of candelabra.

Near the middle of the room was a gigantic geared machine emitting steam and vapor, possessing countless controls, pedals, and keys.

"Let me explain," she said.

"You'll do your explaining from the floor," asserted Billy, his eyes dead set and stern.

She exhaled and grew still.

Irma immediately forced open their captive's mouth and extracted a cyanide pill, intact.

"Tell us, why? What is the reason? Please!" importuned Sovann.

Acquiescent at last, she held a calm face to them, ready to detail her actions.

"I built this machine because I had lost my son to the Workers' City. He had offended the Master of Metropolis by smuggling workers out from beneath and away from Metropolis. He had succeeded in securing the safety of almost a hundred people. Jurgen Fredersen then sent his spy to find out who was responsible, and caught my son. He was then sent to the Workers' City after they had surgically altered his face to look like every other worker face, grim, dour, tired. They had done this to prevent me from finding him, for I am one of the city's renowned scientists."

Sovann, Irma, and Billy were struck by the revelation.

"My name is Dr. Gantrow, and it was I who created the paralyzing rays. I wanted revenge on the whole city, on Jurgen Fredersen, on his spy, and wanted to cease the suffering of my missing son here in the subsurface. I wanted to cease the suffering of all of those who lived and toiled their lives away in the Workers' City. If I could not find my son, then I wanted everything to just cease.

"I built this machine, and discovered my suffering increasing because of loneliness. I have been here with my assistant, whom you have paralyzed by my own invention, and realized I couldn't live the rest of my life without company."

Irma reasoned with Dr. Gantrow.

"Dr. Gantrow, what you have done is noble. Yet, it is not right for us to decide the fate of all of the lives around earth. There are many good souls who are currently bound from doing anything. There are virtuous people, decent people, who do not deserve this."

"My son," was all she said, as her pain started to flow down her cheeks.

"It is not right that the whole world be frozen just because of one person. That cannot be."

They released her from the ground.

Sovann reached out his hand and she held it, his hold bringing her to her feet, then softly she embraced him, wailing out her agony on his shoulder.

She gradually moved to the machine.

All of them watching Dr. Gantrow, all three of them entranced, she performed a complex series of motions on the controls of the machine, completely stopping the steamy haze from emitting. The machine was now dormant.

"Metropolis and the world are now restored. You are right, I cannot stop Metropolis for my own selfish reasons. And I, like you, cannot live without companionship. To be the only people left on earth brought in a loneliness of the likes which we have never felt before. It was the most disintegrating form of loneliness, beyond the loneliness that mortals should ever experience."

She still held Sovann's hand as she stood before Irma and Billy.

They could hear the crowd roar above, as if there was no cease to the constant activities of the Workers' City and the city of Metropolis.

They could hear the moving of the trains, and eventually, while they sat there, they could hear the Heart Machine and the Geyser Machine in operation. They waited in a hush till they heard the ten-hour whistle calling the workers to their ten-hour spells of machine work, its sound reverberating so every Metropolitan received it.

Sitting on a sofa carved from a block of deepest tanzanite, she further expounded that she had aimed the rays in the sky at their airship hoping to knock out everyone in there.

"What your Professor posited was exact. The rays were emitted from my machine here in a V-shape, with the machine and this castle, your ship was within the V-shape, being at the foot of the V-shape. That is how your zeppelin escaped the rays and how you, Sovann, had also escaped. You had barely escaped, Sovann, as you were on the very edge of the ray pattern that wrapped around the entire earth. That is why you were knocked unconscious on the top of the New Tower of Babel and not petrified."

"We must escape now," said Irma. "We must find the restored Professor and his airship and fly from the city before they discover that you have overtaken Jurgen Fredersen's castle and that we have basically sacked the city in the interim. They are bound to ask us questions."

Closing her eyes, Dr. Gantrow was led away from the concealed fortress through the Workers' City, avoiding the surprised looks of the moving workers. She kept calling a name, but her son was submerged among them, location still unknown.

Aboveground, they found the ship, and Professor Saavedra gently led them into the airspace above Metropolis.

"Well, I'll be the son of a bastard. Everything's jake again," beamed Zellde.

✛✛✛

Realizing that she would never find her son again amongst the workers beneath the nonstop movement of Metropolis, she found herself growing closer to Sovann.

As their closeness developed, she was able to revisit Metropolis and find a place to live with him. Since she could not recover the love of her child subjugated below, she found a love in Sovann that filled the emptiness.

In due time, Dr. Gantrow eventually begat Sovann a son, a rosy-cheeked boy.

"Rosy cheeks. Look at him, Sovann! Our son."

She cradled him in her arms, looking out on the golden air of the setting sunlight casting a supernal, ethereal glow on Metropolis.

"The Germanic word 'rot' means red, and the word for cheek in the same language is 'wang.' Also, if you rearrange the letters of my name, Gantrow, they form the name Rotwang. Let us call him Rotwang if you agree, my dear husband."

Sovann said that the name was perfect, so cheerful a name for his own child.

Gantrow, Sovann, and their new child regularly visited the skies with Professor Saavedra and enjoyed the company of their lifelong friends, Billy, Irma, and Zellde. Being and time had returned, flowing, stirring, and as rapid as the progress of the city of the future's future, a city they called their home.

THE END

ON "AND METROPOLIS IS PARALYZED, MOTIONLESS":

etropolis—a city cleaved in two, two halves of a full picture: a city where one half depends on the other, a place where the mediator must be between the head and the hands. In what is possibly one of the greatest silent films in cinema history, just the name *Metropolis* conjures for science fiction fans a whole other destiny and an otherworldly prospect. Being such an enthusiast of this film, I enjoyed writing my story a generation before the generation pictured in the film. I kept the 1920s era argot and parts of speech, reread Thea von Harbou's original fiction masterpiece and also the lesser known likely inspiration behind Lang and Harbou's *Metropolis*, the novel *City of Endless Night* by Milo M. Hastings, a story serialized in *True Story Magazine* from May to November, 1919. Intriguingly, the time at when the clocks stop in *Metropolis* is 3:17 a.m. While writing that section of the story where Sovann sees his pocket watch stopped at 3:17 a.m. was actually around the time of 3:17 a.m. (I like to write in the very early hours of the morning. Why, you may be asking, constant and amazing reader—well, it's the calmest of times and there are no distractions, of course.) After I wrote the story, I also went to see if there was anything unique about the number 317. I discovered that 317 is a prime number and therefore has no divisors. 317 is only divisible by one and itself. Only two divisors. Could this be a symbolic representation of the aboveground and the underground polarity of *Metropolis*? Could it be fate or coincidence? It was coincidence. Calculators may now relax. Influences that seeped into the narrative included the Brothers Grimm story of "The Princess Who Was Hidden Underground" and the newly rediscovered Argentinian footage of *Metropolis*, found in 2008. In one of the newly recovered scenes, Worker 11811 is in a taxicab and fliers are cascading mesmerizingly for the night spot Yoshiwara during his ride. If paused on the Blu-ray, you can see the adages printed on the flier that 11811 reads, epigrams from Omar Khayyam and Wilde. I weaved in a maxim from Seneca for Sovann to read. Also, I intertwined in the spy concept as shown in the newly recovered *Metropolis* scenes, a parallel character known in the Thea von Harbou novel as Slim and in the Lang film as The Thin Man. A fun property of the integer 11811 from the movie: it reads the same backwards and forwards, making it a palindromic integer. Lang and Harbou must also have been keen on math. The characters in this prequel discover that materialism does not bring them ultimate happiness and find that experiences are worth more to them. I found this to be such a contrast to put in the narrative because the characters from the sky are absolutely hedonistic while Sovann isn't. It takes the world to stop for the scientific characters from the zeppelin to learn that it's the immaterial that brings happiness for them. It was a true pleasure to visit a *Metropolis* that existed before Rotwang, Joh, Maria, and Freder. And the mediator for this story? The mediator must be between the material and the immaterial for these characters.

May time in *Metropolis* continue forever.

✝✝✝

DEXTER FABI - Dexter Fabi is a visual artist and writer from the Chicago area. The many hats he has worn include teaching English as a second language in Japan, being a college teacher in California, maintaining an online store of rare and vintage books, and being an information technology administrator for a company in downtown Chicago. After receiving his Master of Science from DePaul University in computer technology, he worked in the industry for years until becoming an educator. Working in the mediums of digital and handmade art, he has exhibited his artwork in the Midwest and in Europe for the World Science Fiction Conventions in Kansas City and Helsinki. He has garnered awards for his art, including an award of First Place in The Waukegan Public Library's Ray Bradbury Creative Contest for Visual Art in June of 2015, held by the very same library that Bradbury himself visited and loved as a child growing up in Waukegan, Illinois. He continues creating for art shows every year. In the course of his writing, he is also the recipient of the literary award of Best Short Story for *The Royal Wedding of Oz* at the annual Winkie Convention presented by the International Wizard of Oz Club. Among his many hobbies are Egyptology, cinema, genealogy, languages, folklore, baseball, pulp fiction, listening to music, and reading, his eternal obsession. He lives in the suburbs of Chicago and is a full-time substitute teacher in local high schools.

THE SERPENT IN THE ETERNAL GARDEN

CARSON DEMMANS

The history of Metropolis says that Joh Fredersen built Metropolis from the ground up and was its sole architect.

The so-called history was written by Joh Fredersen. It was then revised, updated, edited, denounced as a forgery and then rewritten by Joh Fredersen. There is some truth in it. There was, for example, a place called Metropolis, and in that place there was a district called the Club of Sons. People built Metropolis so that some parts of it were much nicer than others and so that a very small percentage of those people would have a much better life than the rest of them.

Other than that, don't believe it.

The Club of Sons was built by fathers who had spent their lives building the foundations of the industrial monster that would become Metropolis. In some cases, they literally spent all of it until their lives were bankrupt of everything and they had borrowed against the lives of their children by depriving them of anything even faintly resembling a childhood. Not only had they been deprived of any meaningful time with their parents, they had been raised in what was essentially a giant construction site with nobody to supervise them. Machines that were meant to bend, melt and cut steel could to the same to young flesh at a far greater rate than it could to metal. Thousands of children died horribly, and even more were crippled, and even more than that were scarred emotionally by witnessing what had happened to their playmates. It was this last group that were the most pitiful as they should have been able physically to live normal lives but their horribly maimed psyches would not let them.

By the time the neglectful fathers had realized what they had done to their sons, it was too late to prevent the damage or even repair it. They could do nothing to make their sons feel better, so they attempted to make themselves feel better. They built the Club of the Sons to heal their own guilt and it worked perfectly. The fathers felt they had done all they could do when the Club was completed so they did no more.

The mothers of these sons were forbidden from being involved in the Club of Sons. Their husbands interpreted the mothers' resignation on this point as their admission of defeat. In reality, it was part of the secret triumph they achieved in establishing the Club of Daughters, which was so well hidden that even the men who built the skeleton of the beast that became the monster known as Metropolis knew that it even existed. The story of the Club of Daughters remains to be told in another tale.

From the beginning, the Club of Sons was a paradox. It was a thing of perfection created by imperfect builders for imperfect members. It contained residences, theatres, athletic venues, massive kitchens and distilleries, and servants. Many, many servants.

The need for servants was a major problem when the Club was first opened. Metropolis had thousands of workers, but they were all involved in constructing the city, both men and women. The fathers who founded the Club knew that they could not expect members of their own class to become servants there, so they were forced to look in the classes below. There was no shortage of volunteers, but they did not fit the vision of these founding fathers. They wanted perfection for their sons in all aspects of their lives. The volunteers who were most eager to work at the Club were from the lowest classes of the workers: the children of unskilled laborers who had grown up in the harshest of conditions, eating whatever food their mothers could find and cook in what little spare time they had. Before they could even be considered for positions at the Club, they had to be properly fed and brought back to something resembling good health. Then, children who had never received anything even resembling an education had to be taught how to serve aristocrats they had not only not known even existed but who lived lives they could not even imagine. One meal at the Club for all of it members resulted in more food being wasted than was consumed by the residents of the underground industrial complex below Metropolis for a week. The homemade liquor made underground was incredibly strong but lacked the decadent taste and aroma of the finely crafted wines and liquors the new servants were trained to make and serve. The very existence of these spirits baffled the first generation of servants. They knew that their parents drank to mask their physical and mental pain; to forget their troubles. Why would the residents of this paradise ever want to forget anything about their lives?

The physical appearances of these first-generation servants were another problem. Their complexions were pale from having lived in darkness most of their lives, and sores, scars and blemishes on their skin was an epidemic. There were no true beauties to be found, so the founding fathers realized that they had to make some.

All of the female servants were gathered and studied closely. Shoes with heels of different heights were assigned to each of them so that they would be the same height. Diets were custom made for each of them so that their weights would all fall in a range so that with carefully designed clothing they would all appear to be about the same size. Their faces were carefully examined and measured in every possible way, and those measurements were then averaged. Each of them then received a detailed makeup regimen consisting of varying layers of foundation and cosmetics. Hair was dyed and colored contact lenses were issued. The final result was not as uniform as they had hoped, but one of these master builders was an architect who had learned long ago that all buildings have flaws; you just have to find ways to mask them. With humans, the solution was obvious: All of the women were issued individualized masks that averaged out their facial features.

The end results were women who were appealing but who had no individual characteristics. They appeared to be machine created duplicates of an ideal that only existed as a blueprint and not a real person.

The founding fathers could not have been happier with this result.

Because the women of the Club were not supposed to be viewed as individuals, nobody ever bothered to learn their names. They were all supposed to be identical and interchangeable, and ultimately, disposable and replaceable, the same as any component in the machines of Metropolis. But like any well-designed machine, accidents happen. In the case of the Club of Sons, the accident was the only female servant to ever be referred to by its members by a title. To them, she was the One. No further designation was necessary as it was obvious who the title referred to. She was, in the eyes of these favored sons, a happy accident.

In her own mind, she was not the One. She was Rebel. Growing up, so many people had called her a rebel that she had taken it as a name. Her rebellious nature had ended any chance of her ever being a drone worker in Metropolis, and the only other option was for her to seek a place in the Club. Even rebels have to eat and have a place to live, and the Club offered a life far greater than the one she had rebelled about.

At first, she tolerated the lessons taught to her and the other girls. The minimum standards were easy to meet, and she had no urge to distinguish herself in serving men she did not like. She felt she had found a way to beat the system that she loathed.

She felt that way until the lessons on makeup and appearance began. She had always been proud of being a square peg that could not fit into any round hole. She had never dreamed that with enough layers of filler, properly moulded, that she would appear to be a round peg. It was an illusion, and did not change her true self, but nobody in Metropolis cared about the inner nature of a cog as long as it fit in the machine and the machine performed properly.

Begrudgingly, she learned how to apply her makeup. Pock marks were filled and scars were evened out. Once a smooth surface was achieved, new subtle contours were added to make her features uniform with everyone else's. Then color was added: cheeks were rouged, lips painted red, and where unruly natural eyebrows had once existed but had been shaved off, new perfect ones were pencilled in. The Major Domo examined them incredibly closely at the beginning of their training, using a magnifying glass to compare each girl with the artificial ideal set out in schematics he treasured as if they were gold. Rebel hated the false face she was forced to wear that made her appear to be yet another perfect porcelain doll to come out of a mould.

She hated it until she realized that if she looked exactly the same as everyone else, nobody could identify her as the criminal who had committed the crimes that she planned.

✛✛✛

All of the servants at the Club of the Sons were trained to act delighted at all times, to anticipate the wishes of the guests, and to provide everything in excess. If the guest was drinking, the serving girls were to bring him his next drink before the current one was done. Second helpings of food were served so promptly they were almost done simultaneously with the first. If one of the fortunate sons was alone with one of the girls in a locked room, it was always the male who begged to be let out of the room.

On the day of her first attempt to become an outlaw, Rebel was assigned to serving drinks. One girl worked furiously mixing cocktails and the others continually picked up the mixed drinks and delivered them. All of them wore identical costumes which revealed their bare limbs and false smiles which revealed their highly whitened teeth. With the constant flow of alcohol, nobody noticed when Rebel emptied the contents of a small pouch she had stolen from one of the many kitchens. The Club of the Sons was always stocked with all spices available for the gourmet meals that were served to its customers, and Rebel's pouch contained the foulest combination of them that she could think of. She left her full tray on one of the tables surrounded by a group of the sons, and her arrival and departure went completely unnoticed. It was several minutes before the sons started drinking from Rebel's tray, but only seconds before one of her customers turned a bright shade of purple and spewed his drink as far as he could. Everyone was aghast, and all eyes turned to the drink mixer. The Major Domo, however, had been carefully supervising the preparation of the drinks and swore that her performance had been flawless.

One of the other youths sitting at the victim's table sniffed the victim's cup and then carefully took a small sip. His face turned a similar but lighter shade of purple before he burst out laughing.

"Couldn't you smell how foul that was?" he asked the victim. "If you couldn't, my friend, then it is a sign that you should have stopped drinking a long time ago!"

"So, you agree that it was meant for me? That someone here means me harm?" the victim complained.

"You are always the first one to finish your drink and take another drink or two before the rest of us finish our first drink, so of course it was meant for you!" his friend chided. "But I don't think they meant you any harm! Whoever did it was obviously looking out for your best interests when you refuse to do so!"

"I don't drink that much," the victim muttered, but he could tell by the looks on the faces of his friends that they did not agree. "But perhaps I should have something to eat and lie down for a while."

With some difficulty, the victim stood up and staggered off. Another serving girl beat Rebel in her efforts to serve him food as well. She dared not smirk outwardly, but her inner self smiled mockingly at her victim.

"One of the servers must have poisoned my friend's drink" a youth at the victim's table said sternly. But, his stern expression quickly melted into a wide grin. "I have no idea which one of you did it, but many thanks! You may not have anticipated his wishes, but you anticipated all of ours perfectly."

Rebel looked at the Major Dom out of the corner of her eye as she grabbed another tray full of drinks. He did not look at her directly but looked at all of the girls with approval.

Rebel's inner self scowled for the rest of the day no matter what expression her face showed.

Alone in her room that night, Rebel began the tedious job of removing her makeup. It began with a strong solvent to dissolve the sealant that prevented any of the cosmetics from running or being smeared during a hard day's work. Then, an oil-based product was used, with a new cotton swab being used as soon as the current one was saturated. The entire process took dozens of the swabs. Then, copious amounts of soap and water were used, and then pure clean water. This was followed by group exercise, although each girl had an individualized regimen in an effort to get them all to the same point of perfection. They received their rations of food and then showered again before applying moisturizers and going to bed.

If she was still living in the underground system that supported Metropolis, she would still be at work at this point in her day and would receive half of the amount of food, if she was lucky.

Luck, Rebel thought to herself as she heard the door of her room being locked from the outside. *Strange how that word doesn't mean what I thought it meant when I volunteered for this duty.*

Rebel was on drink service detail the next day, armed with an even more potent combination of spices. Her plan would not a work a second time, however. All of the youths were certain that they would be the next one to receive a noxious drink, so they were all sniffing their drinks and taking small sips before they dared take a normal sized drink from their glasses. Her inner self screamed in frustration as she laughed at some inane remark one of the youths meant. Her training, as well all of the other girls', included learning how to carefully listen to the tone of the voices of the sons. If the remark sounded like it was meant to be funny, the girls laughed regardless of what words were said.

The sons were being far more moderate in their alcohol consumption than they had ever been, not wanting to arouse the wrath of the poisoner who had struck the day before. The identity of the poisoner, however, was a popular topic of conversation.

"But it couldn't be one of the servants!" the previous day's victim insisted. "Think about it. Their only purpose is to serve us. They are no different than the machines of Metropolis. They have a function they are designed to perform, and they perform it perfectly. Does a spring or a pulley ever decide to deviate from its purpose? Of course not!"

"Perhaps it was an accident," one of his friends theorized. "After all, machines break. One of the girls must be broken in some way."

"That was no accident!" the victim said sternly. "The only way that vile concoction got in my drink was if someone had made it ahead of time and put it in my drink. Look around you!"

The youths looked around at their surroundings. They had become accustomed to the beauty around them and were usually oblivious to it. At that moment, they looked at the lush garden of tree, flowers and shrubs that they relaxed in.

"Breathe deeply!" the victim commanded, and his friends obeyed.

"Do you smell anything resembling the swill I drank yesterday? Do you see anything that could have accidentally soured my wine? I assure you that whatever combination of ingredients I was slipped yesterday, it is not found in nature!"

"Well, if not the servants, and not the Major Domo as he is above reproach and our protector, who could have it been?" asked another son.

The victim looked around himself with a suspicious look.

"On of us?" his closest friend asked with surprise.

"Of course!" the victim concluded. "One of you thought that my reaction would be funny."

"I don't know about that, old friend, but after the fact we all did!"

After that comment, Rebel joined in with the laughter that filled the garden from both patrons and servants. Even the stern Major Domo allowed himself a rare chuckle, and the girls laughed with genuine hilarity for once in as long as anyone could remember.

Except for Rebel, whose laughter proved that in an earlier time she would have been one of the greatest actors who ever lived.

At the end of the shift, the Major Domo insisted on all of the girls disrobing in his presence. Such inspections were supposedly to check the girls for flaws of any kind, but Rebel suspected it was the closest thing to a perk that the Major Domo's job had. Unusually though, he was paying more attention to their discarded clothing than their nude bodies. Normally the girls had their eyes shut for these inspections, but now they all looked on curiously. Rebel flinched as he found her hidden spice packet.

"So, it was you!" the Major Domo said triumphantly. Then, he saw something suspicious in the pile of clothing next to Rebel. He discovered a second pack of potent spices on the second girl, and upon a complete inspection, more than half the girls were carrying contraband.

"When something is done once, it can be funny!" the Major Domo snapped. "Upon repetition, it is tedious! If for some reason one of you decides to act in this way in the future, do it differently!"

Rebel planned on doing so. She planned on doing it so differently that she would not be caught.

✝✝✝

Having decided that it was one of their own who had played the prank with the spices, practical jokes became an epidemic at the Club of the Sons. Having convinced themselves that only one of their own was capable of perpetuating such a brilliant and hilarious act, the sons began trying to outdo each other in tormenting each other with spiked drinks, tacks on chairs, the occasional hotfoot, and various wardrobe malfunctions. However, no epidemic ever reaches an infection level of one hundred percent, so some of the patrons were not amused at being the butts of such jokes and reacted violently. Looking for victims that could not fight back, the sons turned their focus to the servants, with all of the girls laughing mechanically as they were tripped, doused in

THE SERPENT IN THE ETERNAL GARDEN

various liquids and otherwise humiliated. The Major Domo finally intervened not so much to protect the girls but their clothing, which was having to be replaced at an increasing rate. The girls were disposable and easily replaced, but those silk garments were not.

The Major Domo held an unusual position at the Club. He was employed by the Club like the girls, and therefore technically he was a servant of the sons. In practice, however, he was indispensable and without him the sons might actually become responsible for something, even if it was something as personal as their own pleasure. In any event, the attention spans of the sons were at best limited, and their memories were more so. The rash of practical jokes was soon forgotten.

For a time, Rebel amused herself by continuing to pull pranks on the unsuspecting sons, knowing that they would only blame each other. However, as the threats of repercussions by the Major Domo increased, even the densest of the sons began to suspect that it was not one of their own who was the prankster. The girls were still not suspects as they were not thought capable of independent thought. The male servants were given more privileges that the women, so were thought to lack motive. In reality, some of the heterosexual male servants had more to resent the sons abut than anyone, but if anything, they were more motivated than the women to stay in the club. The average life span of a male servant at the Club was more than double that of their worker fathers, and when they did die it tended to be far less painful and violent. The sons came to the right conclusion about the male servants for the wrong reasons, which was still better than their usual reasoning.

"There must be an interloper!" the sons declared. "Someone is intruding in our domain and tormenting us!" The Major Domo was dismayed. He had originally come from the working class himself and lacked formal education. He did, however, have an excellent understanding of mechanics, cause and effect, and what was possible and what was not.

"An interloper?" the Major Domo asked in amazement. "He would have to be intangible in order to breach our security, and invisible to walk among you unnoticed."

"Exactly!" the sons cried in agreement. "As soon as you see such an invisible man, grab his intangible body1"

The Major Domo and the servants froze in unison. Logically, the words that were just said should have been a joke that they should laugh at, but their training told them that their inflection meant that the words were perfectly serious. The sons mistook the silence as a sign of the stupidity of their listeners rather than their superior intelligence.

"If you are incapable of catching this interloper, you must hire additional security!" the sons demanded.

"You are right of course," the Major Domo said blandly. "Having twice the help will make achieving the impossible twice as easy."

The servants glanced at each nervously but silently. They were going to need additional instruction on what was and wasn't a joke. Apparently, so did the sons, as they all heartily agreed with the Major Domo.

Rebel frowned to herself, and this time it was not her inner self who did so. She quickly corrected her error, but realized that nobody had noticed it. In some senses, she was invisible, but only to the oblivious sons. Trained security officers would notice any of her attacks on the sons and her joyous reaction, no matter how subtle. In any event, she had felt some guilt over the mistreatment of her fellow servants. She did not like any of her coworkers, as they all displayed the same lack of personality in private as they did on the job. She had been surprised that some of them had actually planned to copy her spice prank, but she soon realized that if she had not done it first, none of them would have followed. Machines were good at making copies, not originals.

She considered doing something blatant to one of the sons, but it would result in her dismissal. Dismissal was a euphemism comparable to children being told that their pets were being put to sleep. Servants grew soft working in the Club, and upon returning to the lower levels they were either quickly killed in work accidents, or died from exertion, or suicide. Death and suffering were not her intention, at least not her own. Truthfully, she did not want to kill anyone, even one of the sons. At least, that was her original thinking.

One day she was commanded by one of the sons to accompany him to one of the private rooms. She complied. She did not like doing what she was told to do in the private rooms; none of the servants did, but they took comfort in the fact that these tasks took far less time than the work they did outside of the rooms.

She stood there, alone with the son who selected her. She had noticed him before, or more accurately had noticed how some of the servant girls acted around him. Their facial expressions remained frozen around him but the eyes of some of the girls betrayed fear and loathing toward this youth.

She continued standing before him, smiling, awaiting orders. He said nothing, and instead struck her in the stomach with all of his might. Rebel doubled over, more in shock than in pain. He roughly pushed her toward the bed, and by pure reflex she resisted. He was enraged, and slapped her across the face. She paused for a second and then replied in kind, backhanding his face with her right hand as hard as she could.

Before she began working at the Club, Rebel had already begun taking part in the hard manual labor that was expected in the lower levels. She brought

"...you must hire additional security."

heavy metal parts to the technicians who used them to replace broken parts in the machinery and carried away the broken parts. In any given day she carried more weight than any effort any of the sons might exert in a week. The sons engaged in exercise only as sport as they wanted, and not as forced to do so sixteen hours a day. Muscular development was discouraged on the servant girls, but it could not be eliminated entirely in their training. And, no amount of training could ever remover the ability to endure pain that all members of the lower levels developed at a young age. The son's blow stung her and enraged her, but it caused only minor injury. Her blow caused only slightly more injury on the son than she received, but he was totally unaccustomed to pain. He screamed. He cried to such an amount that if he had been a baby on the lower levels he would have been smothered so his parents would not lose valuable sleep for such a trivial matter.

The Major Domo quickly came running. Only he had keys that could open any of the private rooms. Some of the sons followed him out of curiosity, but not concern. They thought nothing bad would ever happen in their sanctuary. The Major Domo opened the door and looked at the injured serving girl and son.

"She struck me!" the son screamed. "Kill her! I demand that somebody kill her!"

Rebel waited her fate with resignation. All commands by all sons were to be followed immediately.

✝✝✝

The collected sons looked at the scene in dismay. They did not particularly like their peer in the private room but also could not understand the actions of the servant girl.

"Did you tell her to do that?" one of the sons finally asked.

"Of course not!" the attacker replied.

"Then why did she do it?" another son asked innocently.

"If she struck you, why is she the one bleeding?" another son asked. "It would seem to me that if she hit you that you should be the one that should be bleeding, not her."

In response, another son struck the speaker in the mouth and watched closely as the shocked son began to bleed from the mouth.

"He's right!" the experimenter declared. "He is clearly the one who has been hit and the one who is bleeding. I'm not bleeding at all. Therefore, the girl must be the one who was struck, and not the other way around."

"An easy enough mistake to make," the bleeding youth agreed, happy to be the victor in this particular battle of wits despite the price he paid for his victory. "After all, there were only the two of them in the room and therefore there was a fifty per cent chance he'd be wrong. Not very good odds at all, really. It also explains the scream we heard. It was clearly the scream of a girl, not a man. In fact, it sounded like a girl much younger than this servant. That is why I came when I heard the scream. A small girl could have been our interloper. If she was quite small, she would have gone unnoticed, almost if she were invisible."

The gathered sons looked at each other with admiration. Logic was clearly the game of the day, and they were all willing to play despite a complete lack of experience.

"She is bleeding because I hit her!" the attacker said angrily. "I hit her and then she hit me and I screamed!"

"Oh damn," one of his comrades sighed. "That makes even less sense than the whole little girl scenario. Why did you hit her?"

"That doesn't matter! I can hit her if I want! We can do whatever we want to these girls!"

There was hushed silence among the youths who had responded to the scream.

"Strictly speaking, I don't think that's right," one of the other youths said slowly. "The laws of the city still apply here. I am certain that there is a law of some kind against hitting other people. Therefore, you couldn't hit her. I think there is a rule that she can hit you back though. Can anyone confirm this?"

The youths shook their head sadly in response. The game had moved from pure logic into a test of general knowledge. Generally speaking, they knew nothing.

"The servants are not to be harmed in any way!" the Major Domo said with far more emotion than anyone had ever heard in recent memory, which meant it had not happened in the past thirty seconds. "Anyone who violates that rule can be expelled from this club for life! That is one of the powers your fathers gave me!"

"You have powers?" one of the sons asked brightly. "Can you fly?"

The Major Domo prepared himself to answer the question in the flattest, most serious tone possible.

"Yes," the Major Domo replied. "But not when asked to do so."

The sons nodded in approval.

"All right!" the attacker snapped. "I should not have hit her! But what right did she have to hit me?"

"The girls are supposed to anticipate our needs, aren't they? And do what we want before we even ask?" one brawny youth said slowly.

"Of course," the Major Domo replied.

"Well, that settles that!" the brawny youth continued happily. "I wanted her to hit him. I've been wanting someone to hit him for some time, so if anything, her reaction time was a little slow, but she did such a good job of it that I think that makes up for her tardiness. Quite frankly, I suspected he'd been hitting the girls for some time so I hadn't hit him myself. If I had hit him myself, there would have been no repercussions. After all, we hit each other all the time, like when we box or do other sports."

"This was not a boxing match!" the attacker said angrily.

"Then let's have one!" the brawny youth replied with a broad grin. "She shall box you. It should be an even match. I've seen you box and you're horrible. I don't think she's had any formal training, but she seems to be in good physical shape. I'll give her a few pointers and act as her corner man to coach her as we go. Why don't we all meet at the boxing ring in an hour?'

"I am not going to box her!" the attacker replied in a high-pitched tone which definitively repudiated the theory that a little girl had screamed earlier. Some of the sons maintained for the rest of their lives that this didn't prove that a little girl could not have been present though, and was therefore the invisible intangible intruder they would look for unsuccessfully for the rest of their lives.

"All right then," the brawny youth said. "You will box me. See you in an hour."

"Or face expulsion from the Club of the Sons for life," the Major Domo said harshly.

The attacker looked at the crowd of sons facing him. He had far fewer allies than he had expected in the crowd. He decided to take the option that would be the least painful to his body and his social standing.

"I'll fight the girl," he said sourly.

An hour later, Rebel and her attacker met in the boxing ring. He wore boxing gloves and trunks. Rebel was dressed in her normal serving girl uniform, including her mask, with gloves. The brawny youth had been very pleased with her athleticism. She had quickly learned the first basic lessons of boxing.

The bell rang and Rebel pounced on her opponent. He was shorter than her and had a scrawny physique. She hit him with a tremendous punch with her right hand, putting all of her weight behind it. Her opponent fell down with such force that he hit the canvas with as much force as she had hit him with. He was not unconscious but appeared to be so because he was using all of his will power to not scream in pain. The response of the crowd of sons was enthusiastic if misplaced.

"Well done!' an audience member said as he heartily slapped the brawny youth on the back. "Great effort in training her so well!"

"I would have liked it to have gone a little longer," the brawny youth admitted. "I taught her quite a bit more than that."

A small minority of the audience, though, was focussing their attention on Rebel.

"Do you think all of the serving girls can do that?" one of them asked aloud.

"I don't think so," his friend replied. "I know a little about that oaf she just knocked out. He has beaten more than one of the girls in the past. None of them must have ever hit him back or we would have heard his screams. Plus, her face showed pure hatred when we all ran to the private room after she hit him the first time. And now, in the ring, she showed real determination. At best, the other girls laugh and smile at us. This one seems to be slightly different than the others."

"Different? Is that allowed?"

"It's inevitable. If you look closely at the girls, there are slight variations in their size and variations. It's subtle, but real. It is the same as a product being built by one of the machines. Due to slight variations in the raw materials that are put in, and the conditions the machine is operating under and its state of repair, there are going to be slight variations in the finished product. I think the raw materials in this girl are different than the others."

"Different? Better or worse?"

"It depends on your point of view. Her opponent would say worse and her trainer would say better. I think better. What do you think?

"I don't know. Still, I suppose your theory makes sense. The girls do move slightly different from each other when they are all moving at the same time. I have noticed that. Actually, I rather like that."

"No, it only makes sense. After all, it's quite like that little girl that's been spicing our food. She can become invisible and intangible. Some people are just capable of doing things others can't. Among the serving girls, she is the one."

And that is how Rebel became known to the sons as the One.

✠✠✠

After the boxing match, Rebel did something which was even more amazing than being noticed as an individual by the sons. She caused the other serving girls to show that they had personalities.

The girls gathered as a group before each shift to receive specific assignments from the Major Domo. They had learned how to see beneath each other's makeup and masks to recognize each other as individuals, even if they never socialized with each other.

"I liked what you did yesterday," one of the girls whispered to Rebel. "In the boxing ring. I was serving drinks to the sons as they watched but they were all distracted when the match started so I watched too."

"I didn't like it!" another girl hissed. "We aren't supposed to distinguish ourselves from each other!"

"You mean like using padding to make it look like you have the largest breasts of all of us?" Rebel said sarcastically. Her critic remained silent and most of the others giggled. They all went silent and stood at attention when the Major Domo entered.

"Rules were broken yesterday," the Major Domo began. The girls flinched, expecting that some or all of them would be fired.

"The sons have been reminded that they have to follow some rules," he continued. "There are actually very few rules they have to follow so hopefully they will remember all of them, for a while at least. They can not injure you, and that includes anything that happens in the private rooms. I am not pleased that one of the sons was struck, but they have interpreted it as something you girls were supposed to do, so there are no penalties for any of you. However, you can not always count on that if you choose to act in a way you are not told to do.

The girls gasped audibly. They were told that they had a choice in some matters.

"Acting surprised is one of the things you are not supposed to do," the Major Domo said dryly. "You should have known that you have always had choices. You chose to come here. You choose to stay. You can choose to tender your resignation. All the choices you make are some variations on those three, but you aren't going to know which choice you have made exactly until the consequence occurs."

The Major Domo proceeded to make assignments for the day. Other than Rebel, all of the girls had made the decision to not do anything that might result in their dismissal. Essentially they were going to be doing what they had always done, but they took a strange pride in actually making that decision.

Some of them took the extraordinary step of actually making a second decision. They decided to keep a watch on Rebel. They had a strong suspicion that it might be entertaining to do so.

Rebel had decided that she was going to follow the rules that day. She had no desire to end up in a boxing ring again with any of the sons, including the one she had beaten the day before. The sons tended to repeat behavior they enjoyed and they had enjoyed watching her fight. Without anything to trigger their limited memories though, she hoped the memory of her actions would quickly fade. The other girls shared her hope. They knew the sons could not tell them apart and did not want to end up in a boxing ring being mistaken for Rebel.

As the day progressed, more and more of the sons congregated in the gardens of the Club. For the most part, they had already forgotten what had happened the day before. However, none of the serving girls had forgotten, and no matter how hard they tried they could not stop themselves from looking at her from time tome. Some were hoping she would do something unusual and the rest dreaded the possibility. The subconscious minds of the sons functioned far better than their conscious ones, and they could not help but follow the glances of the serving girls. In the end, everyone in the garden, both servants and sons, were looking at Rebel. She did not care in the least and went about her duties as if nothing was wrong.

The Major Domo was going to do something to correct the situation, but realized that this was the easiest way he had ever seen to amuse all of the sons at once. They ate and drank less than normal, and were quiet and well behaved.

However, the sons continued to eat and drink at a decreasing rate as they spent all of their time looking at Rebel. This meant there was less and less for the serving girls, including her, to do until they were all at a standstill, not moving.

"Why are we staring at her?" one of the sons finally asked.

"She must be the One," one of the philosophers from the previous day answered.

"One what?"

"The One," the philosopher explained. "The girl from yesterday that slapped that oaf and then beat him unconscious in the boxing ring."

"Are you sure?"

"Of course!" the philosopher reasoned. "Why else would everyone be looking at her?"

The problem with nonsensical reasoning is that it can come to the right answer despite the best efforts of the people using it. The murmurs went around to all of the sons as to Rebel's identity, and it was overheard by some of the serving girls. Normally they ignored the prattle of the sons, but having nothing else to do they had been listening in. It may have been something as simple as a few knowing glances or a few nods of various head, all done subconsciously, but the actions of the girls reinforced the conclusion as to who Rebel was.

The Major Domo finally grew bored with supervising a group of statues and said "Does anyone want anything? Anything at all?"

"Yes," the philosopher answered happily. "I want to know if that serving girl standing alone over there is the one from the boxing match yesterday."

"You are not allowed to know the identity of the girls," the Major Domo said grimly. "That is one of the rules."

"Well, I went so far as to read those rules you mentioned yesterday," the philosopher said smugly. Everyone in attendance gasped. The sons could not believe that one of their own would go to such effort, and the servants could not believe that one of these brainless youths could read.

"The rules say that we aren't supposed to know the servants' real names," the philosopher continued. "Well, I don't want to know her real name, do I? I want to know if she was the girl in the boxing ring yesterday."

"Why?" the Major Domo asked cautiously.

"That doesn't matter," the philosopher replied. "The rules say that my requests, if reasonable and not against the rules, must be granted."

The Major Domo gritted his teeth, not believing that he had just been outwitted. He promised himself to replace this latest craze, logical thinking, with something less harmful to the club, such as orgies.

"I am," Rebel said. "I am the girl from the boxing ring yesterday."

The Major Domo glared at her, but she shrugged.

"He was right," Rebel said. "His request was reasonable and within the rules, so I honored that request. Now that we have settled that, would anyone like some drinks? Food? It would be more interesting for everyone involved than everyone staring at me."

The One had proven herself to be an expert in entertaining the masses so the sons followed her suggestion. Rebel than began an intricate plan to conceal her identity. Whenever some of the girls were gathered in a group for any reason, she would join the group, obscure herself from view, and then wander off in another direction, using other girls for cover whenever she could. By the end of her shift, she was sure that none of the sons would know who she was. She was correct, but hadn't anticipated the consequences that it would have.

The next day, the self-styled philosopher arrived in the garden with a black garment. It was a replica of the uniform for servant girls, but black instead of white.

"Which of you is the One?" the philosopher asked. The Major Domo was furious.

"No names!" the Major Domo said angrily.

"It's not a name," the philosopher said shrewdly. "It is a title, just as you are the Major Domo, the servants are servants and the sons are the sons. I am not allowed to know her name, but I can give her one, or in this case, a title. This

"I am the girl from the boxing ring yesterday."

black uniform will identify her at all times."

"Why?" the Major Domo asked.

"So, if she does something wrong, we will know who she is and who did it, and not blame you or the other servants," the philosopher said sweetly.

The servant girls needed no further instruction. Half a dozen of them grabbed Rebel, stripped her, and redressed her in the black uniform before she knew what happened.

One servant girl, however, was not pleased, and planned her revenge.

The servant girl glared at Rebel and her new black uniform. Just as Rebel had named herself Rebel, this girl considered herself Beautiful, and Beautiful is how she referred to herself when she thought of herself, which she often did. Of all of the girls, beautiful was the one who required the least makeup in order to meet the look of what the Club had deemed the perfect look for the girls. She needed no hair dye or colored contact lenses, and had to use little more than some lipstick and a small amount of rouge to get ready for work. Her skin was clear and unblemished, and her figure was pleasing and required no padding, even if she did use it sometimes in an effort to gain more attention. She did not even have to wear high heels. She had volunteered to work at the Club because she enjoyed receiving attention, and working in the Club instead of underground would help protect her looks.

Rebel went about her duties in her new uniform. She decided that if wearing it was the worst thing that was going to happen that day, it was not going to be a bad day.

She was wrong. It was an extremely bad day.

Beautiful was serving drinks, but doing so absent mindedly as she was watching Rebel whenever she could. She took a misstep and spilled dark red wine all over her white uniform. She was furious.

"Look what you made me do!" she accused Rebel.

"I didn't make you do anything," Rebel sighed. "Get changed or you'll get into trouble."

"Why?" Beautiful demanded. "Because then you'll be the only one who looks different again?"

"No," Rebel sighed. "Because those uniforms are valued more that you are. If you have it washed quickly, it might be able to be saved. If you don't, neither it nor you will be savable."

"Don't tell me what to do!" Beautiful hissed. She took her stained uniform off, and stood naked in the garden.

"There!" Beautiful proclaimed. "My uniform is off, so you should be happy. And now, I'll make sure that we both look the same!"

Beautiful grabbed Rebel's black uniform and pulled it off easily. The black uniform had been made using the pattern for the white ones, and the white ones had been designed for the convenience of the sons, who had trouble unwrapping packages at the best of times.

Rebel was angered, but not embarrassed. She picked up her new uniform, and was pleased that it was torn. Now she could go replace it with a traditional white one. If she was lucky, the philosopher who had gifted it to her would become distracted by a bright shiny object and abandon the idea.

Beautiful was not to be denied her vengeance, however. She made a violent if ungraceful charge at Rebel from behind, succeeding in knocking her down. Children in the underground had no toys, so when they did play it was often rough and physical. Beautiful had never engaged in roughhousing, but understood the basic principle of making contact in some way with someone else.

Rebel's knowledge of roughhousing was far more advanced. She did not want to hurt Beautiful, or anyone else for that matter unless it was necessary, but she had been a rebel when a young girl as well. She had spent most of her time playing with boys rather than girls. Wrestling was a common game, and she had not cared if she always lost when she was younger. As she grew older, she was forced to become more proficient as her all male opponents developed instincts other than just winning. They enjoyed touching her more every year she developed, and before she volunteered to join the club it had become closer to self defence than sport.

Rebel rolled over onto her back, and when Beautiful bent over to grab her, Rebel grabbed both of Beautiful arms and planted one foot firmly into her stomach. She was then able to flip Beautiful up and behind her. When Rebel got up, Beautiful was still flat on her back from the flip. Rebel did not want to turn her back on Beautiful again, so she began backing up slowly while she watched the prone girl. She was shocked when she was pushed roughly from behind. She looked behind her at the coward she had beaten in the boxing ring.

"Wrestle her!" he demanded. "I am not ordering you to hurt her, but if I could be forced to box you, then you can be forced to wrestle her."

Rebel looked at the Major Domo in dismay, but the older man shrugged. Apparently having her and Beautiful fight was considered to be a reasonable request. At least their beloved uniforms wouldn't receive any more damage.

While Rebel had silently pleaded with the Major Domo, Beautiful recovered and launched another attack from behind and tackled Rebel to the ground.

She grabbed a large handful of Rebel's hair, and looked up with surprise when she heard a shrill whistle.

Everyone turned and were surprised to see that the brawny youth who had served as Rebel's boxing coach had now appointed himself a wrestling referee as well. He was holding a metal whistle and began barking orders to the combatants.

"None of that!" the referee said authoritatively. "You've seen us sons wrestle each other, so you know the basic rules. No striking of any kind, no choking and no hair pulling. No scratching or biting. Begin."

Rebel and Beautiful looked at each other in confusion. What had started out as a temper tantrum had involved into a major sporting event. Beautiful had little athletic ability, but heard cheers when she managed to escape one of Rebel's holds or manage to take Rebel down. Even if she was sharing the spotlight with someone, it was with only one other girl and not dozens. Beautiful grappled with far more enthusiasm and the sons began to refer to them as the One and the Other. It wasn't as glamorous a title as Beautiful, but at least it was a title.

Rebel fought on, but with little enthusiasm. Her superior skill allowed her to block most of Beautiful's attacks, but she did little else. Beautiful got her into a clinch and whispered into Rebel's ear.

"Fight back!" Beautiful demanded. "Would you rather do this or serve wine we can't drink and food we can't eat? At least we're doing something!"

Rebel accepted the fact that they were going to battle until someone declared a winner. She gave into Beautiful's momentum, but reversed her position as they fell so that she landed on top of Beautiful. She remembered vaguely that being on top of an opponent meant something in the sons' sanitized version of wrestling. She was right, and the referee held up her hand in triumph.

"To the stadium!" the referee announced. "More competition!"

There was little response to his challenge, and what little there was, was negative.

"Not us!" the referee clarified. "The girls! We'll watch them compete! That was quite thrilling!"

The girls smiled with their mouths but their eyes showed a complete lack of thrill with that decision. Then, the referee turned Rebel around to face her and gave her a large goblet of wine. She looked around for who she was supposed to give it to.

"It is yours!" the referee announced. "To the victor goes the prize!"

Rebel glanced at the Major Domo, who was giving free reign to the new enterprise until he saw what the result was. She drank her wine with gusto. It was not the finest that the Club had to offer, but it was far superior to the home brew that was the only available alcohol in the underground. Servants were normally not allowed to drink or eat what was available for the sons, and alcohol was forbidden. She finished it in several gulps, much to the delight of the sons.

"Fabulous!" one of the sons cried. "We shall have the girls wrestle, race, jump, and do all the events we normally compete in! And, the winners shall receive wine!"

"What about food instead?" one son suggested. He was fonder of wine than all of his comrades combined, and was always afraid that Club would run out.

"They can have their choice," the referee said as a compromise. He began organizing events. The servant girls were a little leery of the prospect, at least until that they saw that the sons were actually carrying food and drink themselves rather than making the girls do it. The prospect of being served by their masters was too tempting, so the girls competed as hard as their bodies allowed. There was a silent agreement among the girls that they would let each of them win something, and the sons did not seem to care. It was a better day then most, but Rebel now felt she was being looked on by the other girls as a leader.

She had no urge to lead. Being the head sheep still meant that she was a sheep. The only other option was to run.

✝✝✝

"I quit," Rebel said bluntly.

She was standing in the Major Domo's small office. It consisted of a large desk in a small hidden room and many towering stacks of paper work. One of the Major Domo's many tasks was to manage the finite resources of the club so that it appeared to the sons that its resources were infinite. Food and drink inventories were carefully monitored and new supplies had to arrive shortly before the old one ran out so as to not overflow the storage area. Mundane things such as offices, warehouses and janitor closets were all located behind hidden doors in obscure parts of the Club to maintain its utopic appearance. It took a lot of work to convince the sons that work was not necessary in life.

"No, you don't," the Major Domo said with no emotion in his voice. He never raised his head or took his eyes off his paper work.

"I have a choice to quit or not!" Rebel exclaimed angrily. "You said so yourself!"

"I said that you could choose to tender your resignation," the Major Domo said, his head still down. "You have chosen to do so. However, it is my choice as to whether or not I accept your resignation. I do not. Shut the door on your way out, shower to get the stench of sweat and competition off you, go to your room and put on clothing before you come out of it again. Thank you."

Rebel looked down on her body. She had not even realized that she had remained nude after Beautiful had pulled her black uniform off. The uniforms themselves left all of the limbs of the wearer bare and were so light that girls did not even realize they were wearing them. Apparently they also did not realize when they were not wearing them. She was stunned. She had not been the subject of any unusual attention as a result as all of the sons were concentrating on whichever girls were competing in each competition. The servant girls were expected to anticipate the needs of the sons but it was like trying to predict what combinations would result from ten dice being rolled at once. There were too many possibilities and no logic as to what might happen next.

The Major Domo looked up from his desk as he had not heard the door open and shut.

"I will be thankful when you leave, but not if you stay," he said sternly. "Your resignation has been rejected. If you attempt to leave, guards will stop you. The guards are not members of the Club. They were recruited from the lower levels as you were. They will not collapse after one punch like a house of cards made out of paper tissue."

Rebel could clearly hear the disdain in his voice.

"You despise the Club members?" she asked.

"I like my life here," he said with a sigh. "I come from the lower levels as well. I was not as far down as you were, but I assure you my life was not much different than what was common for you and your family. I like where I live and how I live. My job allows me to have this life. Everything in Metropolis is a product of a machine, including the machines themselves. The Club of the Sons is a machine. The purpose of the machine is to produce happy patrons. I do not have to like the product of the machine in order to enjoy operating the machine."

The Major Domo dropped his head down again and concentrated on his paper work. Rebel turned and left and followed his instructions and ended up in her room as she had been instructed to do.

After that, she only did what she told herself to do.

She put on a fresh uniform and mask, but not her makeup. She kept her head down as she made her way to another secret room. It was a janitor's closet. The janitors were not meant to be seen by the sons, but they were issued drab uniforms that would attract no attention if one of the sons saw a janitor by accident. The janitors themselves were small, unobtrusive men who would draw no attention either, so she was able to fit into a spare uniform. It was a little big on her, but not noticeably so. She found several large plastic bags and made her way to a kitchen.

Servant girls worked in the kitchens as well. Even though the kitchens were also hidden from the sons, the girls were required to wear the same uniforms, makeup and false smiles that they were always expected to wear. One of the girls looked up as Rebel was filling her bags with food.

"What are you doing?" the girl asked. Rebel kept her back turned to the girl and tried to lower voice.

"As I was told," Rebel said. The girl shrugged. She had sufficient supplies to do her job properly and without criticism, so she had not really cared what the janitor was doing. She preferred working away from the eyes and hands of the sons, and as long as nothing interfered with that she did not care about it. By the time Rebel left the kitchen, the girl has already forgotten about her encounter, and when asked about the deficiency in food inventories she could honestly tell the Major Domo that she did not know how it had happened.

She had thought of many possible ways to get out of the Club but they were all risky. She would likely injure or kill herself if she tried to scale any walls or breach any of the exits. Instead, she went directly to an exit that was obscure but guarded by a single security officer. She walked up to him directly, but keeping her head down. She dropped one of her garbage bags of food in front of him, and opened it so he could see the fruits, vegetables, meats and baked goods it contained. Like the servant girls, the security guards did not eat the food that the sons did. The guard looked at the bag curiously.

"This is for you," Rebel said in her lowered voice. "I am leaving with the rest. If you ask no questions, you will have no idea if I am doing anything wrong or not, and you will be able to eat what you want and hide the rest before you are asked what happened. If you stop me, we will both get nothing."

Most of her speech was wasted. After she had said the dropped bag was for the guard, he had dropped to his knees and started going through his newfound wealth. He had heard that the Club routinely threw out perfectly good food and as far as he was concerned he had simply seen proof of it. When asked later if anyone matching her description had left, he answered that he hadn't, and theorized that it was the invisible intangible little girl everyone was talking about. She easily stepped past him and went on her way.

✝✝✝

What exactly her way was had yet to be determined at that point. The upper levels of Metropolis were well lit and populated. It was far less densely populated than the lower levels, but it was also policed. Below, only the machines were protected, but here everywhere was policed and monitored. She was able to find another hidden janitor supply room. There were signs to look for if one knew what to look for. Inside, she ate heartily. She had been on strict and tasteless rations for months.

She stopped for a second and pondered that last statement. How long had she been at the Club? She suddenly realized that she had no idea. Nobody was allowed to record time in any way, and there were no calendars or anything else to suggest how much time had passed. She had not aged noticeably whenever she looked in a makeup mirror, but her skin was also constantly covered with chemicals to prevent it from showing that. Had it been months? Years?

In any event, the food was delicious. Even uncooked, the vegetables and fruit were delicious. She decided that she should concentrate on the bread on cooked meat she had taken first as it was likely to spoil first. She had served sandwiches to the sons but had never actually tasted one. She was surprised at what a clever invention it was. Some bottled water finished her meal. She had taken wine as well but saved it. She expected that she would need it to bribe or barter with any resistance she met or help that she needed.

She had wondered how she would be able to reach the lower levels. When she had been brought up from the lower levels to work in the Club, it had been through an endless system of heavily locked staircases that were separated by great distances. She finally found the last stairway she had been led out of, and was surprised that on her side; the door was unlocked and easily opened. Apparently the elite of Metropolis had never thought that someone might actually want to leave unless they had ensured that they had the keys required to come back.

She still wore her janitor uniform so people did not give her a second look. She found a place to hide as she ate. A child wandered by and looked at her bags. Rebel was prepared to offer the boy a piece of fruit, but after a few seconds he simply shrugged his shoulders and left. He had never seen fruit and vegetables before, so he did not even recognize it as something that he might want to eat.

Rebel looked cautiously around the level she was on. It was better lit and ventilated than where she had come from. These people were the technicians who controlled that apparatus that made the upper level so luxurious: power generation, water purification, heating and other utilities. She had no idea how to begin to do that work, and her requests to be taught only made people suspicious of her. If she belonged there, she would have been taught since birth how to do the work. She was suspected of being a loafer rather than an intruder when found sleeping in a storage area asked and was told to wait for security to arrive from the upper level.

She bolted from her captors and was pursued until they saw where she was running to. She was going to a stairway that went down another level. They had no concern about the well being of those below, only those above and themselves.

Rebel continued downwards over a period of weeks. She had run out of food and her uniform was tattered. Her location looked vaguely familiar and spun around when she heard a familiar voice. It was a boy she knew as Wrench because his grip as a wrestler was like a pipe wrench. When she saw his face, he was startled. He had aged horribly, and had scars over most of his face and exposed body. He did a double take when he saw her and finally asked her a puzzled question.

"So, you are dead after all, are you?" he asked.

Rebel shook her head. He was not convinced.

"You look the same as the last time that I saw you, and ghosts don't age. Only people. Besides, all of your family is dead, so it makes sense that you would be too."

"How did they die?" Rebel asked. She had no real affection for them, but she had hoped to find shelter with them. Wrench scratched his head in reply.

"I don't know if anyone knows. Nobody saw it. Explosion of some kind, I'd guess. Their home was destroyed with them."

"Will you help me?" Rebel asked.

"No," Wrench replied.

"We were friends," Rebel said.

"Yes," he agreed. "But how can I help you? If you are a ghost, you need no help and can't be hurt. If you are not a ghost, you are far better off than I am. How could I make things better for you? There is no room for you to stay or food for you to eat."

Rebel's training as a servant had already started to fade and her face showed sadness.

"You had forgotten, hadn't you?" Wrench asked. "What it was like, here?"

Rebel nodded.

"There is nothing I can do for you. You always tried to find your own way. Where did it lead you?"

She began talking about the life she had led and the places she had seen. The concept of the upper levels was foreign to them, and the concept of the upper level was totally incomprehensible. How could such wonders exist?

As she talked, people gathered around her, fascinated.

"You must be lying!" one little boy said. Wrench slapped the child hard, In the Club of Sons such force on a young boy would have resulted in great penalties. Down below, the only surprise was shown by Rebel, and then people

"You had forgotten, hadn't you?"

around her at her surprise.

"She has never lied to me!" Wrench said angrily. "I remembered when she left here, so she had to go somewhere, didn't she? Others have left but never come back. She has always done things her own way even if it made no sense to me. I would not have come back, but she did."

"Well," said the boy's mother, "there is no more time to talk today anyway. Come with me. You can sleep with my family and I will make sure you get something to eat. Tomorrow you can continue your story."

"I will?" Rebel asked.

"If you stay here, you need to work," the old woman said. "Nobody else can tell the stories you can, so that can be your job. Obviously, people want to listen."

There was now a full-fledged crowd around Rebel, all straining to hear her speak. For the next few days, she carried on as a story teller, wandering around the level. It may not have been entertainment, but it was not work, so people listened. Eventually, people stopped her from talking.

"We have heard all of your stories," the old woman said. "You must go."

"Are there levels below this one?" Rebel asked.

"I have no idea," the old woman said. "We were told you were coming and how to have you taken away again."

The old woman raised her hand in a signal and a man saw it. He blew hard into a whistle like the ones she had seen in the Club. Out of the shadows came security guards, some of them holding strange machines she had not seen before. They were big men, and were approaching her menacingly. She feigned a retreat and then stepped forward as she threw a hard punch as she had been taught for the boxing ring. The man went down. Another guard grabbed for her and she ducked. Lashing out her leg, she swept his leg out from under him and he fell hard. She performed the same wrestling flip that she had done on Beautiful in the Club on her next attacker, but she was outnumbered. She saw a familiar face in the crowd of workers surrounding her.

"Wrench!" she yelled to her old friend. "Now you can help me!"

Wrench nodded as he left the crowd as he approached her from behind. He grabbed her from behind and held her tightly by her arms. She knew that she could never break his grip.

"What are you doing?" she screamed.

"Helping you the only way I can!" he said harshly. "You are not a ghost after all and I don't want you to become one! They took you away once and you lived. Let them take you and you might live again. If you stay here and fight you won't!"

Rebel stopped fighting. She had tried to find a life without constraints and had found out that there were just some bonds that were softer than others. The only escape was death, and she had never wanted that.

"Take me away," she said softly. "How did you find me?"

"We always knew where you were," one guard explained. "The machines pointed at you aren't weapons. They send pictures of you back to the Club of Sons. We have followed you since the night you left. One of the sons recognized you as the One and knew you would do something worth watching. Your journey has been the only thing they have talked about since you left. When you had no where else to go or do, we were told to bring you back."

"Why?" she asked. The guard scratched his head.

"What do you mean?"

"Why do the sons want me brought back?"

"They wouldn't know if I asked them," the guard said with what might have been a laugh but sounded more like a bark from a well-trained watch dog. "You know that. They only know what they want. They want you."

Rebel lost herself in thought as she was led back upstairs. Apparently logic was no longer the game of choice among the sons. She thought back to the private rooms and how many men would want to take her into them. She shuddered at the thought of what the new game might be. There was always a game, and girls never won.

✛✛✛

She was brought back into the Club of Sons by the guards. Anything that the guards said to their superiors was lost in a chorus of loud cheers. Among the cheers was something that resembled a chant, and she strained to understand what it was.

"The One! The One!" some of the sons yelled.

One what? she thought. *Victim? Criminal? Hero?*

She laughed at the last suggestion she had made to herself.

She was led to the room where servant girls made and repaired their uniforms. Normally there was only the familiar white fabric available, but today there was a wide variety of fabrics in different colors except white. The Major Domo entered, looking unimpressed.

"Make yourself a new uniform," he said. "The sons want it to be different than all of the other girls, but you are to choose its appearance."

"Why am I here?" she asked in exasperation.

"Your resignation was rejected," he said with a slight smile. "In the eyes of the sons, you never left. They think that everything you say and do is for their entertainment. They had you followed and watched everything you did on giant video screens they had put up in the stadium. They cheered every time you escaped and laughed every time you were in a fight and hung on every word you said and movement you made."

"So, they saw what life is like below?"

"They saw," the Major Domo admitted. "But they don't believe it is real. Don't you see? The only thing they know is this Club. They love you more than anyone else because everything you do is a surprise to them. They think somehow that you created this amazing entertainment spectacle for them and have no idea how or why you did it. Don't you see? The only reality they know is this Club. You could slaughter one of them in cold blood tomorrow and someone would say they had always wanted someone to do that and then carry on with their day."

Rebel stared at a pair of scissors she held in her hand. She knew that if she stabbed herself that she would die, but she had fought so hard to protect herself all of her life that she wasn't capable of self harm. She considered the Major Domo's suggestion of murder, but quickly discarded that idea as well. She turned the pair of scissors around in her hand and began cutting material for her new uniform.

She spent days in the sewing room, being brought food and water regularly by other girls. She was surprised that she was receiving the food and drink that the sons usually received, but received only polite, false smiles in reply. She was also being treated by the girls as if she was one of the sons. Whatever she was, she was no longer one of them.

She was not a great seamstress, but the simple black dress that she wore on her first day back in the Eternal Garden caused a sensation. It was long and dignified, and had sleeves. She wore no makeup and her hair was pulled back off of her face. She did little that first day except sit and watch others. She in turn was watched by the sons, but she instructed the girls to carry on as they always did. The sons had been conditioned to eat and drink as food and wine were brought to them, so they continued on as they normally did.

The next day was more shocking than the first. Rebel was dressed in all seven colors of the rainbow in an outfit that was anything but dignified. Her top was tight and tiny, squeezing her figure in a manner nobody had dreamed of. Her skirt was similarly tight and short, with colors brighter than the light coming into the garden. Her makeup was thick and grotesque, a mockery of what the serving girls looked like. Her cheeks were the color of molten steel and her lips similarly looked like fire. The red sat on a thick coat of white foundation. In another time she would have been called a clown. In the Club of Sons, she was simply called the One.

She had resigned herself to becoming the subject of requests from the sons, and her garish appearance was a challenge to them, daring them to pay her attention. She received it, but not as she expected. There were no orders for food or drink or to go to the private rooms. She finally sat beside one of the sons and confronted him.

"What do you want of me?" she cried.

"I don't know!" he said. "You are the One! We call you that because you are the only one like you and you do things we could never dream of. You are one of a kind!"

"All women are one of a kind," she said. "All people are one of a kind!"

They youth looked around himself. Clearly the One was wrong. All of the other girls looked and acted the same. Everything the One did was entertaining, he reasoned, so he should laugh at her comment. He did so and Rebel left. She refused to call herself the One.

In some ways she was alone though. The servant girls refused to communicate with her and the Major Domo did not engage her in conversation other than to communicate such information as where her new living quarters were. The room was luxurious. Her first instinct was to destroy it, but she resigned herself to living there. Out of loneliness, she began engaging the sons in conversation, which delighted them. They did not believe her stories of life in the lower levels, but did not tell her that. She was beyond their comprehension and they loved her for that. On rare occasions she told one of the sons that they were going to a private room, and the son quickly obeyed. She was given unlimited access to the kitchens and the sewing room. Every day she ate and dressed and drank as she liked. At times she gave food and wine to the guards and the servants, and they dutifully ate it. She was trying to make them want more than they had, to dream. She failed in that but succeeded in gaining their affection.

She tendered her resignation repeatedly, sometimes daily. She thought that she could wear the Major Domo down, but she stopped when he finally spoke to her.

"If you were to go, it would be like the last time. There is no place for you elsewhere. You will always end up here. You have more freedom here than anyone else, including the sons who are prisoners of their own feeble minds. What exactly are you trying to escape?"

She returned to the lower levels many times, but now with the security guards and their cameras along side her. She resigned herself to always returning to her plush prison, but continued telling her stories to people in the lower levels. She did not know why. Perhaps the sons were right. Maybe logic was simply a game but nothing more. Maybe life had no logic at all. She was not happy, but on the other hand she felt better than she had before in her life.

Was that good enough? Her rebellious nature told her no, but its voice grew quieter with time.

Her presence was always a cause of delight on the lower levels. Wrench had died not long after her first return to the Club, and it was not long until everyone she had met in her first return visit to the level she had grown up on was also dead. Time passed quickly on the lower levels. In the Club it did not seem to pass at all, and it was only Rebel's everchanging appearance and actions that reminded the sons that time passed at all, and that every day was different.

✝✝✝

There was no way of telling exactly when Rebel died or how old she was. Her appearance changed every day so no slow deterioration was noticed. In any event, none of the sons remained sons forever. They became men, fathers, husbands and then their sons eventually took their place in the Club. As she grew older, her behavior grew more erratic. She visited the lower levels less often, although her adventures there were still broadcast on large screens in full stadiums when she did. She spent more time in her room, alone. Nobody thought to check on her, as the sons wanted to be surprised by her and not find out for themselves what she was doing. It was the Major Domo who finally found her corpse. He was not the Major Domo she had known when she first arrived at the Club. That man had died long before Rebel did, and his replacement held her in greater esteem than the sons did. His job was to amuse the patrons, but she did that more than he could ever dream. To her nonconformity was in itself a norm, a paradox that amazed generations of boys who knew nothing but uniformity and precise design.

The Major Domo was shocked when he found her corpse. It was not the corpse that shocked him, but what she had written on her mirror some time before she died. It was in her brightest lipstick and printed boldly, if not defiantly.

I AM NOT THE ONE

The meaning of this message was debated by the sons. Some thought it meant that the One was not dead at all and this was simply one of the entertainments she created for them. After all, they were talking about it, and talking was fun, wasn't it?

Others thought it was a sign that the dead woman was no longer the One because another girl would take her place. According to legend, she had not been chosen to be the One; she had simply become the One on her own.

The serving girls were watched carefully to see which one of them would distinguish themselves in such a way. However, one of Rebel's legacies was that the training of the servant girls was changed forever; conformity was ingrained in them to the point that independent thought didn't have to be forbidden; it was simply impossible.

In time, the One was forgotten by the sons. She had been loved in her time, but without her constant changes to remind people that it was a new day, the concept of time was forgotten as well. The members of the Club of Sons changed, but the Club itself remained frozen in its state and purpose.

When the history of Metropolis was written by Joh Frederson, there was no mention of the One or anything that could possibly have been interpreted to lead to a theory that she may have once existed. Men who had known her in the Club never spoke about her once their time in the Club had passed, the same as they were forbidden to ever speak of anything about the Club, and her memory there slowly faded away.

In the lower levels, Rebel's legacy was different the lower one travelled. To the utility engineers, she was a cautionary tale to children: if you did not learn your job and had nothing you could do, the only escape was down. At times, a brave child would push open the door of one of the staircases and take a quick look, only to run away screaming that the legends were true and there was a horrible underworld they had to work hard to avoid.

Further down, the cautionary tale shifted in its focus. It was possible for people to come from upper levels and go below, but then they were only led by big scary men to wherever they had come from in the first place. There was no point leaving your station in life as you would always be returned to it eventually. The story of Rebel gave many people a sense of peace and contentment they had never had before.

At the lowest level of the underground, where Rebel had been born and often visited, she was never forgotten. Every story that she ever told about life in the levels above was memorized by as many people as possible, and they regularly tested each other on their accuracy. New stories grew about her, told by people who had known her and seen her on her many visits, and they were taught to all children who came long after her death. The stories were told before bed, at meals and even screamed while working so they could be heard over the machines. She was never forgotten.

More importantly, she was never explained. Unlike in the levels above, there were no morals given to the stories. She was neither the Devil nor Icarus. As she had often told people, she did not want them to be like her; she wanted them to be like themselves. One child who heard the stories became a singer. Nobody had ever heard a song, but he had followed some instinct deep inside himself and he listened to it, singing loudly about whatever he could think of.

Another child became an artist. If the lady from above could make herself look different every day, why couldn't other things look different every day as well? She made her own paints and decorated walls and made portraits of people. The most popular one she was requested was different versions of Rebel. Eventually, she even created her own images from her own imagination. This led to people creating variations of their own clothing, making themselves recognizable and individualistic.

When the population of the lowest level finally realized that Rebel had died and was not coming back, they told stories about how she had affected them and they missed her. This was a revolution in itself. Death was no longer something that was simply inevitable. It was a time to remember people and what they were. Life gained new value when death had significance and people remembered those who had died. Children were watched over so they wouldn't die.

A more subversive element learned a different lesson from Rebel, or at least the men who came with her. They had strange metal objects that opened doors and let them go upwards. There were plenty of pieces of metal on the lower level, so why couldn't they open the doors? Although it had no name, locksmithing became a secret past time. It was forbidden to go to the upper levels, but to some that made it even more irresistible. The lady from above had started where they were and found a way upwards. The fact that they could do it themselves and without men to show them the way was the dream, and when it was finally achieved, it was a sensation. Once there, even more doors were discovered! A never-ending source of illegal pleasure that entertained generations of outlaws until the uppermost was finally breached. Once there, there were no further doors to open, but some cautious expeditions were made, matching landmarks with Rebel's stories. Even the Club of Sons was found, verifying everything the legendary storyteller had told them.

The sightings of these outlaws, even fleeting ones, created new legends and dreams. If there were worse worlds below, could there be greater ones above?

Over time, all of these elements came together. A girl grew who knew all of the stories of the upper level and how to get there, as well as the art of opening any door that was locked. She valued life and wanted people to live their own lives. Unlike Rebel, she was a leader, but without Rebel she would have never existed.

Her name was Maria.

THE END

AFTERWORD

The Eternal Garden in Club of Sons represents, in my opinion, the Garden of Eden. As such, I felt it needed a serpent. In the film and the novel, Maria invades the Garden, but is not really the serpent. In order to match the original story, the serpent has to come from within the Garden. That is how the character of Rebel was created. Like the serpent, she tries to disrupt the idle perfection of the Garden. Unfortunately for her, she has a harder time of it than her predecessor. Everything she does is misinterpreted or limited by her own moral compass. Instead of casting people out of the Garden, she tries to escape herself, and fails again. She is able to live out her life under her own terms, but is unable to bring down the Garden and the Club of Sons, at least in her lifetime.

Although there is no bloodline between them, Rebel serves as an ancestor of Maria, creating a framework that will eventually lead Maria to invading the Garden with the children of the underground. It is not the immediate result that Rebel wanted, but the original serpent probably never anticipated all of the consequences of his actions. If the original serpent had not created the situation that resulted in Adam and Eve being expelled from Eden, Mankind would still be in paradise and Jesus Christ would never have come into being.

Rebel is not a hero. She is a disruptor. As shown in how different legends build up around her actions, the people of the different levels of the underground interpret her actions to suit their own purposes. It is only the people at the lowest level who interpret her as some sort of inspiration or savior. They are wrong, of course, because Rebel does not see herself as a leader, and rejects that role. Still, if she had not acted in the manner she did, Maria would not have the inspiration to rebel against the horrible conditions of Metropolis. She succeeds, but only because she succeeds in finding an ally in the Garden, something Rebel is never able to do.

The patrons of the Club are shown as nameless drones. What few differences they have in reference to each other are minor. Like the servant girls at the Club, they resemble goods mass produced by a machine rather than individuals. They also interpret Rebels actions to suit their own purposes: they consider her to be an entertainer whose only purpose is to surprise them with her antics. They can not believe that any of the servant girls, who exist only for their pleasure, would actually want to cause mayhem in their paradise. Some of them will probably spend the rest of their lives searching for the invisible intangible little girl who must have been responsible.

This story is not canon. There are a thousand other possible explanations for the events in Fritz Lang's film and his wife's novel. Like any works of art, a thousand different people are going to interpret them in a thousand different ways.

✠✠✠

CARSON DEMMANS - is a freelance writer in Regina SK, Canada. Since 1994, he has been published more than 1500 times, with sales varying from a single sentence for cartoon gags to newspaper columns, magazine articles, and short stories. He is the author of four books so far, with more in the works. The first three are regional humor, but his most recent one is OH MY GOD! THEY PRINTED THAT?, a history/satire of sexist and racist comic books. If you like books about pop culture history, check it out on Amazon or at Bear Manor Media. He needs the money.

MOVERS OF THE EARTH

HARDING McFADDEN

They say the plague came in on the heels of a red-shoed wizard. They say lots of things.

Alfred was hardly nine when Maria had taken him in hand, him and a dozen other children, and led them up, up, up into the unbearable light of civilization. They'd trolled through corridors cleaner than the tables that he'd eat at in his life, to doors greater than the height of his home, and had come out into that unbearable, unbreakable light, into the Club of the Sons, into the beautiful faces of the great and mighty. She had pointed, and insisted, "Your brothers!"

Your brothers, he'd think later. What a farce; what a lie; what a tragedy. But he'd wanted to believe, they'd all wanted to believe, because they'd wanted to believe her, because of her sincerity, her surety, her beauty. And so they'd believed, and they'd gone, and they'd seen, and they'd been expelled.

Like so much trash down the bottomless shoots to God only knew where, they'd been expelled, the oldest of them to the youngest, and while the guards hadn't been rougher than they'd needed to be, they'd nevertheless been firm. Thus, they'd come up, up, up to meet their *brothers*, and had been expelled again, down, down, down, into the shadow-filled underworld where men sweated and bled and oiled the machines, working as the arteries of the arteries of the great Metropolis.

Alfred was hardly nine when he'd met his *brothers*, when he'd realized that there was no brotherhood of man, but rather separate species of mankind, and that some had no humanity in them at all. He'd seen the world fall, and the beautiful Maria crumble, and the lunatic fall from his great heights. He'd seen the white hair flash, and had heard not a single sound as the lunatic had fallen to the lowest levels of the topmost world. He'd seen what happened when the mediator between the head and the hands let go of one of its charges, and those very same hands turned the crank on the great meat grinder of the world. And...

And...

He'd seen something lower. Something altogether unexpected. He'd seen the residents of lower hells, still, that had reached out dutifully for the earthly remains of a madman that had had the world held tightly in his synthetic fist.

✠✠✠

How he'd found himself in the world above, on the street just below the spires and arches of the great cathedral as the body of the madman had struck the earth with thunderous force, he couldn't afterwords say. Though there he was, in a fog of consciousness, watching as the life's blood of the wild-haired lunatic had seeped into the asphalt and blacktop; as the robotic fist had clenched and unclenched as if with a mind of its own; as the chalk-white hands of things no longer altogether human had greedily reached from the shadows for those same remains. There he was, seeping into those same shadows, his shocked mind thinking back over the past few moments...

When the great tumult had erupted, the children had awaken with fear, sure in their childish way that the darkness was alive, and that what roiled in it brought with it the end of all things. Alfred had crept from the squalid safety of his thin bed, had calmed his sister, Brigitte, one year his junior, where she cried in the bunk above his own. Across from them in the shadows perched their parents' bed, half again as wide as theirs', the bed things every bit as threadbare, and absolutely empty.

Helping Brigitte down from her bunk, he'd sat her on the end of his own, and instructed, "Stay here. I'm going to look for Mamma and Papa." Yet when he'd turned to go, she'd latched onto his arm with her terrified little clawed hands, and begged him not to leave her alone. With a sigh, he nodded, took her hand in his, and led her out of their sleeping room, and into a world gone mad.

Rounding a corner, and exiting out into the main streets through which the adults trudged, he'd been just in time to see his Mamma and Papa going up the last lift out, his mother shouting about how every man and woman was with them. In her madness, she didn't seem to notice, none of them did, that they'd all left their children behind.

Seeing their feet disappear into the sky, Alfred took notice for the first time of the shifting and shuffling behind him. Turning to look back, he saw the other children for the first time, dozens, hundreds, of them, crowded together, closer than kin in their fear.

Though hardly the oldest one there, he was still the calmest. Taking the burden upon himself to keep the others calm, he'd looked into countless wide, terrified eyes, and smiled, disingenuously, and said, "Don't worry. They'll be back. They'll be back. You'll see." His voice sounded small and hollow to his ears, but that hardly mattered, just as long as the others believed him.

Their belief was short-lived, as in seemingly no time at all, came the flood. The great deluge flowed from the roofs, erupted into the streets, and instantly the other children were screaming mindlessly, panicking, and he couldn't fault them for it. After all, he'd panicked, too.

But then had come Maria, and thereafter her man, one of Alfred's *brothers* from up in the sun. Taking hold of their own fear, the two adults had done what they could to pull the children from the waters.

In the gray-shifted lunacy that erupted from inside Alfred's mind, he was more spectator than participant in his own actions. Once nearly submerged beneath the growing waves, trying as he might to shove his sister to the top of the tumult, to give her a few seconds more of life if nothing more, he'd suddenly found himself drifting along on a tide of flesh, through his subterranean world, up a flight of stairs, and out onto the streets of his brothers' city, their Metropolis, its streets gone dark as their spoiled souls.

What happened to the others after that, he would learn much later. In a haze, when they'd emerged onto the darkened streets, he'd found himself one amongst dozens, simply too many for the few adults present to keep an eye on. Without conscious thought, he'd drifted away, mindless, to wander the alleys and side streets that carved their ways between towers and bridges and walkways that pierced the sky, proudly, sinfully, as if begging God Almighty to strike them down!

When the screams of horror had erupted from the beautiful people on the walkways and upper roads and opened windows of the cyclopean buildings, he'd been pulled from his senseless revelries, just in time to see the madman fall, plummeting from the sky like a stone. At first his arms flapped, like he was trying to learn how to fly on his way to the ground. If any could have figured out how to do it, it would have been the madman, Rotwang, but he simply didn't have the time. In the seconds between the tumble and the impact, he'd hardly had the time to think, "Lord, help me!" had he been the type to think of something higher than himself.

Watching the form falling, falling, Alfred couldn't bring himself to look away. In horror he followed the inevitable course of the scientist, sure in an uncomfortable way that when he at last made impact, that he'd pop or explode like an overfilled balloon. But such was not to be the case. When he'd hit, Rotwang had landed solidly, hadn't bounced, hadn't exploded, and for seconds thereafter, until the color had left his face and the lunatic light had left his eyes, he'd still looked alive, if completely broken.

Hardly any others were around, most having moved away from the expected carnage before it had arrived. Stumbling, Alfred had moved toward the remains of the great man, where he'd landed half in, half out of the shadows cast softly by the nearly lightless night. Kneeling, he'd reached out a shaking hand, the knee of his gray trousers turning red from contact with the bloody ground as he'd knelt. Reaching further and further, fingertips mere inches away from the body, he'd wrenched his hand back as the mortal remains of mad old Rotwang began to move.

Throwing himself backward, Alfred had landed on his seat, eyes wide and gawking, sure that if this body, broken as it was, were moving, that the scientist had not been a man, had never been one, but rather had been a devil, alive and corrupting this broken world. Though as he looked into that pallid face, he saw no twitch nor color to signify that life was returning. Instead, it became apparent that the remains, far from moving of their own accord, were being drawn into the shadows that covered fully half of them.

Looking toward those shadows, Alfred barely repressed a shriek when thin, skeletal, chalk-white hands reached out into the pale light, and drug the corpse back into the blackness. Two hands…four…purple-nailed and taking hold of the flowing fabrics of the reddening clothes of the madman, and dragging them away.

✝✝✝

As he moved further and further into the arterial alleyways and roads away from the cathedral, as he distanced himself from the cacophony of the crowds clotted there, the slithering-slinking noises of the white handed strangers grew louder in Alfred's ears. Though still thin and silent, they were the only sounds this night after the denizens of civilization had been left behind. The machinery of life had been stopped. The roar at the cathedral had dimmed with distance, until it had become a whisper, then a notion, and finally only a memory. Now, for all that he cared to notice on that windless night, it was only himself, the shadows, and *them*.

Even during his brief excursion into the lights of civilization, Alfred had never been on the streets of the great city, had never felt the slickness of the new roads and walkways, nor the age-smoothed cobblestones of the older paths. His feet bare, his shoes having been lost without his knowing, the cobbles felt almost soft against his soles. They were dry, and as his still wet feet struck them, it was with a soft slapping sound that was as much imagination as reality.

Ahead of him moved the unseen shadows. Four hands, dragging along one corpse, itself so broken as to no longer be rigid. Two hundred pounds of cooling nothingness, on its way to who knew where?

Down a deep expanse of alleyway he followed the sounds. Perched in an ancient part of the city, things were different there. The ground wasn't uncluttered with litter. There was a smell altogether unpleasant. He could see nothing, but the walls felt filmy under his questing hands and with every inch gained, there came the sensation of delving into something simply old.

Suddenly, with no warning, he came up against the back wall of the alley, bruising his fingers, and stumbling over piles of trash and broken boxes. A nail bit harshly into the heel of his right foot, cutting deep, and staying put until he was forced sit in the trash on the ground and wrench it free. Blood wetted his hands, and as he gripped the foot, a single tear spilled down his cheek.

Sitting quietly for a few moments to gather himself together, he became aware of the lack of other sounds. No longer could he make out the footsteps and dragging of his query. He was alone, and it was oh, so dark.

Yet, where could they have gone? He'd hit the back of the alley. It was hardly a go-through. Standing tenderly, he made a full circuit of the walls, backtracking some thirty feet until he came within sight of the rest of Metropolis again. Nothing. No stairs, nor ladders, no way for them to have escaped. Then how…?

For fully another quarter of an hour, he felt every square inch of the alley, careless of the rotten muck through which he stumbled and crawled. His fingers came into contact with many ghastly things: old, small bones that he hoped were from mice or rats; cylindrical metallic cans that crumpled to dust when he handled them; the nail that he'd stepped on, and another one very similar, sticking up out of a board four feet long, piled among others like it. He was altogether wretched and filthy when he at last found what he was looking for.

When he found the trigger, he was shocked. A thumb-sized bit of moveable stone in the lower left corner of just another brick in the right wall of the alley, it pushed in with slight effort. Depressing it, he shoved and a door, small but more than large enough for a pair of stooping men, opened before him. The light that filtered out was sickly and green, like a bioluminescence in a pool of water that was evaporating and stagnant.

For a long minute he stood there, at the edge of something altogether unknown, unsure if he wanted to continue his trek. His childish fears of the dark, the unknown, death, nearly overwhelmed him. With very little urging, he would have turned tail, and found his way back to the cathedral, to Brigitte, his sister, to Maria and the safety she offered. But then he became aware, ever so faintly, of the clicking of heals, way down there in the darkness, and the sound of a broken man being drug along between them.

For a moment, he again looked back, remembering all that he had known, all that Maria had promised him. He grimaced, disappointed, knowing that he could leave it all behind him right then, and miss very little. He'd been in that world, not of it, as if it had never been his home, and he just a sojourner passing through. In the end, he realized, it was really no choice at all.

Taking a shaking, bracing breath, Alfred entered that green-black darkness, cautiously closing the hidden door behind him.

✝✝✝

The light ....was sickly and green.

The tunnels and stairways through which he moved felt tight, the air heavy. The ever-present sickly green glow overlaid everything ethereally, like he was strolling through a populated nightmare. There was no looking around or down, as the shadows were as dense as lead, but after the first few hundred yards had been traveled downward, the claustrophobia he'd felt began to lift, and there was a feeling of openness just on the other side of his reach.

The flights of stairs on which he traveled were thin rods welded together, a dozen to a step, and green eternity glowed through the gaps. The handrails felt older than old, like they'd been bubbled up from the core of the world at the moment of its creation. Aged paint flecked off under his fingertips. The back of his neck itched with the certainty that there was something behind him, just a few feet back. Time and again he turned on the stairs, terrified, absolutely positive that someone was there, behind him, watching him, reaching out a skeletal hand. Yet, time and again, he'd turn and find…nothing…

He wasn't sure just how long he traveled, moving along walkways that were the horizontal siblings of the stairs, passing through gaps in the walls like holes bored by termites. Though all the while he was aware of the hundreds of thousands of tons of metal that surrounded him, and he wondered who had built this? Who *could* have?

When the stairs and tunnels finally came to a sudden halt, it wasn't up against an impenetrable wall, but rather onto dirt, damp and packed and trod upon. Kneeling, he shifted some of it between his fingers, and held it up to his nose. Far from sterile, it smelled earthy, alive, even down here, deep in the heart of the world.

His eyes adjusted to the minimal light, he looked out over the landscape before him, and gasped. Far from empty, there seemed to be buildings here, some short, others tall, with cobbled walks snaking between them. Neighborhoods, streets, apparently lifeless, with flickering green streetlights still casting their faint glows downward. And above it all, the roof of the world, a rounded concrete sky a hundred feet high.

With cautious steps, he moved his way into the neighborhoods, walking chill streets, through air that was damp and tinged with something unknown. The buildings that he passed were of red brick, and green shingles. Open windows were glassless, the rooms beyond black as the void, eyeless faces looking on from nothingness. He knew that the creatures he followed were somewhere nearby, and that he had seen no other signs of life, but could still not shake the feeling, the dreadful absolute certainty, that somewhere out in all that darkness, something watched him, many somethings, with eyes adjusted to this bleak landscape.

The place was like a fever dream, and yet while he felt anxiety, there was also an accepting calm. Whatever he might find here, he knew, could be no more nightmarish than what he'd left behind him. And so on he walked, deeper into that dream, feeling the roads move beneath his sore feet, carrying him along.

At the end of one long block of houses, situated between two buildings where another street should have been, was an open lot, fenced in, and filled with thin metal and wood structures that sat unmoving like headstones. Coming to a break in the fence, where a gate half hung by a rusted hinge, he entered the lot, and looked around.

The things here were old. Metal rods no thicker than his wrist were twisted into massive half-domes, a pair of triangles connected at the top by another rod, and a short flight of stairs that led to the top of a slide. In his child's mind, some sad ancestral memory told him that these were amusements, meant for children, from a time before the fall of the old world. With infinite melancholy, he ran his fingers along one of the chains suspended from the rod between the pair of triangles, caressed the seat that connected this chain to another. Gingerly, he sat upon the thin seat, and once sure that it could hold his weight, walked himself back, kicked his feet forward, and swung. There was no breeze here, but his movements made one for him. All discomfort and worry vanished as muscle memory that wasn't even his awakened, and he smiled, kicking and dipping, and having something akin to a childhood for the first time in his young life. All conscious thought left him as, for moments all too brief, he simply existed, without a care in the world.

Reaching the forward extreme of his swing, his bubbling laughter died in his throat as he noticed movement out there, in the shadows. The chains creaked as he swung back, his movements ceased, the swing slowly groaning to a stop. Strain his eyes as he might, he couldn't see whatever it was that had caught his attention. He had only phantasm impressions, a body like any other adult, feminine, but thin, skeletal, hanging from it threads of what might be clothing, or flesh. In his mind's eye, it was a horror beyond description. Though in truth, he couldn't have swore to anything actual.

Stepping from the swing, he crouched, shrinking in on himself, as he backed away from the shadow. The fence here had no opening, but he was young, and fit, and in no time at all was scaling the fence, and dropping down on the far side.

When his feet hit the ground, he looked back, and there the shape stood, just outside the sickly light cast by the streetlights, unmoving, oddly familiar, a dead shadow, *watching him.* When that smell reached out to touch his nose, that horrid stink of burnt hair and cloth and flesh, it was altogether more than he could bear.

Unable to control himself, he screamed, all the terror in the world crashing down on his young head, and ran as quickly as he could, away from the lot, the dead memory of innocence, and the shape that he was absolutely certain was following him.

✝✝✝

The streets and alleyways seemed to constrict as he ran down them. Each ragged heartbeat made his vision pulse in and out, as if he were on the very cusp of unconsciousness. His legs were leaden, his chest burned, but he dare not stop. Though he could not hear it over the hurricane sounds of his own rushing body, he was sure, in the way that only children can be sure of things, that the horror was right on his heals.

Leaping a short fence, he landed in the gray grass of a small square yard with a thud, his legs finally giving out, his body shaking and exhausted. Eyes wide with panic, he looked behind him, and was relieved to see nothing there. No silhouetted monster, no shifting shadows, nothing. Only this still, stagnant world.

Pulling himself along more than walking, he moved toward the house that the yard fronted, and sat on a thin porch. Elevated three steps above the yard, it would have been pleasant enough, if not for that ever-present funereal feeling. He sat there for a long while, looking, and catching his breath. Once he'd rested for a few moments, he stood on shaky legs, and looked around. To his right was nothing, simply more porch stretching out to the end of the house. To his left was a porch swing with wood so aged that it looked like chalk held together with tacks. Moving toward the swing, he stopped, seeing on the floor beneath it a pile of old bones that were much the same color as the wood above them. Taking a knee, he looked at the bones without ever reaching out for them, and was saddened to see that they were not human bones, but dog. A good boy, no doubt, who'd laid there to rest while waiting for the return of a master who'd never come home.

Turning from the sad sight, he stopped before the front door of the house, with its torn screen and missing glass. Reaching a careful hand through the empty frame, he groped around until his fingertips brushed the knob inside. Turning the lock, he retracted his hand, opened the door, and went in.

The house was furnished, well-appointed, yet musty. A chair and low couch looked more like cactuses than furniture. Springs shot through upholstery that had long ago rotted out. Splayed on the couch, bones run through by springs, were the bones of a human, no doubt resting where they'd died. The bones of the left hand and forearm rested separate from the rest of the remains on the circular carpet that filled the center of the room. The head was blessedly turned away, toward the back of the couch, the face hidden.

Forcing himself to breathe steadily, Alfred moved through the house, into a kitchen with faded blue and chrome counters, a circular table with enough spots for three to eat, and a cracked linoleum floor. In a rusted rack by the sink were stacked dishes with once pretty blue flower patterns around the rim. Mounted to the walls were glass-fronted cupboards, sagging but steady, their cups mostly matching the pattern of the plates. The wall over the sink had a window large enough to give a pleasant view of a back yard, with the spiderwebby remains of lace curtains hanging over them limply. At a corner of the kitchen was a thin door that led down to a basement, but there his bravery gave out, and Alfred was sure there was nothing that could entice him to go down into those unfriendly depths.

Back into the living room, and up a flight of steps to the second floor he went. At the far end of the hallway that ended the flight was situated the bathroom, with thin wash basin, toilet, and lion's paw bathtub. The floor was light blue and white tiles, the walls papered with matching underwater scenery full of bubbling fish and seaweed and down-drifting sunlight.

The bedroom on one side of the floor was sparsely furnished, the walls papered a pleasant yellow, and the remains of a rocking chair being all the furnishings. It was sad, and somehow fallow, as if it were the seed of a dream that never materialized. With great melancholy, he closed the door and moved across the hall.

The second bedroom was every bit as large as the first, but filled with the ghosts of life. There were dressers and framed pictures and knickknacks galore. The bed was large. Upon it were the bones of a second person, and for no reason that he could understand, he was certain that this one was a woman. She lay there, arm bones crossed over her chest, remains situated securely, lovingly, as if someone had gone to great effort after she'd passed to make sure she was comfortable.

Looking at the framed pictures that lined the top of a short dresser, Alfred's eyes drifted toward one in particular. In it a man and woman, younger than his own parents, and happier than either had ever been, were standing before a building not unlike the cathedral of Metropolis, dressed in exquisite finery. He in a handsome suit of gray cloth, she in a dress of purest white. They held each other like they never wanted to let go, but not as if they were life preservers. More like each was the other's perfect idea of an eternal partner, found against all odds, and completing lives that otherwise would have been left unfulfilled. What they held onto was a waking dream.

Leaving the room as he'd found it, Alfred retreated to the hallway, but before closing the door behind him, he took one last look at the remains on the bed, and for no reason he could discern, said, "You have a nice house. And... I wish you'd been my mother..."

Down the steps and back into the front room, the boy stopped by the open front door and looked out into the front yard, and the street beyond. What had he found here? A world under a world? Filled with the comforted dead and white-fingered body thieves? If not a lower hell, than a middle one? Perhaps purgatory?

✝✝✝

Two blocks later on, he came across a wire mesh trashcan perched precariously, and half eaten by rust, on a corner. The black plastic bag that had worked as a liner was dried and crumbled at a touch. The refuse inside was much the same. There were cans rotted to shells, crumpled bits of random waste, and on top of the lot, the yellowed papyrus of an ancient newspaper. Scarcely able to read, at least anything more complex than manuals instructing in the use of the great machines, he scanned the front page, taking in the black and white photograph that centered the text of a the communal burial site. Lips twisting uncomfortably, he sounded out the headline:

DEATH TOLL RISES AS MYSTERIOUS PLAGUE CLAIMS THOUSANDS

He'd never heard the word "Plague" before, but by context, he could reckon what it meant. He spun in a slow circle, looking at the empty eyed buildings around him, and in a rush understood it all. The dead husband and wife, maybe even the dog on the porch, had been killed along with thousands of others. Maybe millions by the end. Until all of these houses were filled with the remains of those lives, here and all over the world.

Yet it was more than that. This was no lost world within a world, a dark underground where dwelt ghosts. This had been the world once. The upper world, where now stood the mighty, sky-piercing Metropolis, far from being the epitome of civilization, that world above all others was only one more tombstone, built on the tragic remains of what had come before it. It was no great paragon. It was nothing but a ghoul, stripping the life from something earlier.

Dropping the newspaper in the trashcan, he watched sadly as it burst apart like ash, puffs of the past trickling up to tickle his nose. He blamed those particles for the tears that rimmed his eyes.

Walking on, he looked in and around everything he could see. He circled neighborhood after neighborhood until his feet hurt. When at long last his strength had all but ebbed, he sat on a rickety wooden slat and steel frame bench, and wallowed. He'd followed he knew not what to get here, and in truth he wasn't sure if he'd ever be able to find his way back. There was a world around him every bit as full as the one he'd left above, and if the way which he'd descended was the only option, he might die here.

Looking across the thin street from where he sat, he was taken by the sight of the building before him. Columned out front, and having formerly been home to massive windows that reached twenty feet or more high, its peaked roof gave the imposing impression of importance. Above a set of wide double doors a plain sign read **LIBRARY**.

Standing on tired legs, he moved across the road, stopping briefly at a cube of engraved stone in the gray grass before the library. On the cube was what appearing to be a carved picture of a pair of tablets, on which were written a list of ten commandments, though the years had dulled the sharp edges of the letters. Running his fingers over the smooth remains, he was sure that something important was lost here. Something capable of great change.

Climbing the flight of stone steps to the double doors, Alfred stopped long enough to take in the weight of the place. It was like the dust of centuries lay here. The air itself felt thicker, somehow. Filled with memory.

The inside of the building was silent as a tomb. Sagging and broken shelves were everywhere. In neat piles before them were stacks and stacks of books. Hardbound or paper, they were obviously well cared for, even though nearly every spine and cover was more thought than reality.

Walking down the isles between the stacks, he could hear only his own breath, his own heartbeat. There was nothing, but still that ever-present surety that something was watching him.

At the back of the main room was a table which, unlike everything else present, was dust-free. On it sat a single volume, and two stacks of fresh-looking paper. Standing before one stack, he picked up a piece and felt it. Rough to the touch, it was obviously hand made. But by whom?

Taking the top sheet from the second pile, he marveled at the words and pictures there. He'd never seen anything quite like it. Dynamic action illustrated words meant not so much to educate as to entertain. This was no instruction manual, no detailed explanation of the workings of the great machines that pumped the life's blood of Metropolis. Confused, he looked at the volume that claimed the table with the papers, and saw the same words and pictures, though infinitely older. Whoever was responsible for this, then, was not the creator, but the copier, a preserver. Remaking the words and pictures so that they might not be lost to the ashes of time.

Gently, reverently, replacing the sheet where he'd found it, he backed away

...he was taken by the sight of the building...

from the table, and shrieked when a voice that came from everywhere at once told him, "You're not supposed to be here."

In a terror, he turned from the table and ran for the exit, hoping, begging, whatever higher power might exist in this middle hell that whoever had spoken would not take hold of him before he'd made the street, and at least an open kind of safety. Though as he ran, the voice followed him, admonishing: "You're not supposed to be here. This is a sacred place. And you've brought her here behind you. Don't you understand? *You're not supposed to be here!*"

He was through the doors and down the steps and running for all his worth another block, two, three. A mile passed, and he was certain that the owner of the voice was right there. Another mile drug beneath his feet, and at last exhaustion overtook adrenalin, and he began to slow. Blackness seemed to seep into his vision from the outside, pulsing in closer with every beat of his heart. *Lub*-slowing-*dub*-stopping-*lub*-falling-*dub*-oblivion…

✜✜✜

When he became aware of the tickling on the end of his nose, Alfred cracked his exhausted eyes, and saw the spider-thing right there. Five-legged and dragging a hundred tails behind it, it was running a digit along the blade of his nose as if trying to figure out what it was. Rolling onto his back and crab walking away from the thing, he gritted his teeth as it pursued; closing in on him though it appeared eyeless. At a brief distance, he could see that it was not, in fact, a spider, or a bug of any kind. It looked, rather, like a hand, carved of dull black metal, the tails being stringy metallic veins pulled from the inside of an arm. How it was moving without a mind to control it was beyond him.

As it reached his foot, it took hold and began dragging itself quickly up his leg, his shirt, before finally latching onto his collar. Screaming, he pushed at it, not wanting to touch it, but completely unwilling to let it touch him. From it he could feel something more than simple animalistic actions. Malevolence permeated its every movement, gave it a kind of life, leaving him with no doubt that should it take hold of his throat, it would choke the life from him.

Holding the impossibly strong hand by its pinky, the thumb and index fingers clenching at his Adam's apple as the middle and ring fingers gained purchase on the flesh of his chest, Alfred screamed. So engrossed was he by the horror show making haste to kill him, that he at first took no notice of the man moving nearby.

Running up to the boy, the stranger swung a long-handled shovel with both arms, hitting the murderous hand expertly, and launching it away from Alfred.

Bits of tearing pain erupted from his chest as bits of skin were wrenched loose where the hand had held him tight. Another thin trickle of blood flittered down his neck from his Adam's apple where the forefinger had gashed him as it had flown away.

Watching the airborne hand fly through the darkness, he lost it in the shadows some fifty feet away, and the idea of not knowing where it was seemed every bit as unnerving as having it reaching for his neck. It landed somewhere with a thump and a rustle, and was gone from that place. Which left Alfred alone, in the green-hued underground, with the stranger.

Leaning on his shovel like it was a walking stick, the stranger was tall and thin and white as chalk. His eyes were large and dark, nearly black, his hair and uniform clothes ash-gray. Though it was his fingernails that grabbed Alfred's attention most: they were purple, like on the hands that had grabbed the remains of Rotwang.

"Child," the stranger said, leaning toward him. "You're not supposed to be here."

✠✠✠

Keeping what he hoped was a safe distance; Alfred walked parallel the stranger as they moved deeper into the heart of the subterranean town. For the first time, the boy became aware of movement in the shadows that filled the houses. Attic windows that had seemed empty before were suddenly alive with pale silhouettes, dark alleys were home to thin, shambling figures. This was no boneyard. But, was it a community?

"What do you call this place?" he asked.

"It was called Willowview before, as I understand it. But we just call it home."

"Do you have a name?" he squeaked. The stranger chuckled, and it sounded like the rustle of wind through dry leaves.

"Kirby," he answered.

"Kirby?"

"I was named after my grandfather. Not my father, thank goodness. I don't think I'd have survived being called Horace, even though he did. For a long while at least. And what do I call you?"

"Alfred."

"Alfred. That's a fine, a truly fine, name. Alfred. Not many Alfreds down here. None, I should think. But if there's any that I haven't met, there wouldn't be many."

"How many people live down here?" He looked around again, wearily. The illusion of a safe distance was gone. He was surrounded on all sides. If they wanted him, they had him, and he could do nothing about it. Though he felt no antagonism, only curiosity.

"Here? At last count nearly a hundred. Though I've heard tell that in other such places there are more of we caretakers."

"What do you do here, Kirby? What's a caretaker?"

The older man stopped suddenly, face transfixed, confused, as if it had never occurred to him that someone might not be familiar with his job. Looking at Alfred much as one might an idiot child, leaning heavily on his shovel, he gently explained, "What we all do. What our parents, and grandparents, and great grandparents have done since the plague. We've survived, so that we might be caretakers of the dead. Though"—he looked at his feet, his words somber and unsettled—"we've recently failed on that front."

"What happened?"

Looking up into the gathered darkness, Kirby said, "A madman found his way here. From your world. From up in the light. Found his way down into our depths. And he stole the memory of the plague from us."

"I'm sorry, Kirby," Alfred said honestly, and not sure why. "But, I don't understand."

Moving again, the older man explained, "To understand, you'd have to look behind, back, into history, or memory, or myth. Though I'm of the opinion that it's a bit of all three. Though I get ahead of myself. Let me show you something."

Before them was a massive metal fence, the tops dulled spear tips, stretching so far off in both directions that it may well have gone on forever. The gate doors were fifteen feet high, black, and open, beckoning any lost soul to enter. And like the lost souls that they were, Alfred and Kirby entered, followed by the nearly one hundred other denizens of this subterranean necropolis.

Past the gate, the ground moved on in hilly swells and dips, as much like titanic waves as earth. Between the hills ran arterial walkways of the same cobblestones as the roads. Upon the hills, in perfectly spaced lines, lovingly tended, were thousands of headstones, stretching out as far as his young eyes could see.

All was pristine and solemn, the gray grasses expertly cut to the same uniform length. Nowhere was there sign of disturbance or unrest. Except in the center of the tallest hill, where the mound of earth lay.

Moving up the tallest hill, his knees shaking, Alfred looked at the pile of earth, at the purple mound-shroud that covered it almost tastefully. The hole beside the pile was roughly rectangular, six feet deep, a gaping maw waiting for its last meal. Beside the hole, opposite the dirt, was the coffin.

Alfred had never seen a coffin before. His world being what it was, the tradition of interring the dead was something long unpracticed. When the people of his culture died, their worldly remains were thrown into the machines, their usable bits used, their useless parts thrown in with the other refuse. There was no reverence. There couldn't be, as the people themselves were only more cogs in the machines. As such, this whole place, this massive testament to the dead, may as well have been an alien world.

The coffin was a simple thing, of the plainest wood. The lid was on no hinges, but was sitting loose beside the rest, waiting to be nailed in place. Inside the coffin was the body. The earthly remains of Rotwang, the madman, lay almost peacefully. His hair was as frazzled and wild as it had been in life. His face looked much the same, save that all color had left it, leaving it seeming almost hollow. His eyes were closed. He may as well have been sleeping. Across his chest, his arms were crossed. Wait... *His arm*. While his left hand lay comfortably on his right breast, where his right should have been stopped just below the elbow, his heavy shirt torn at the sleeve, as if the hand had survived its master.

Alfred blinked hard. The spider-thing that had tried to kill him.

Circling the grave, Kirby said, "A long time ago, there was a great plague. They say it was brought into the world on the heels of a red-shoed wizard. Of course, they say lots of things. In the end, millions died, all across the world. Everyone lost someone, and some lost all, but as is the way with such things, there were survivors. And while some of them decided that the best thing to do was to pave over the dead world that had gone before, others believed it their duty to see to the proper disposal of the dead. We are the descendants of those that stayed."

The boy looked into the faces around him, expecting still to see monsters, ghoulish creatures that feasted on the flesh of the dead. Instead, what he saw was a sad gathering of people whose ancestors had decided to do the hardest thing. He saw mournful faces that had never seen sunlight, and that stayed because no matter what they did, the job was never done. He saw no fanaticism or monstrosity, but rather a quiet dignity, a heroism of sorts.

Those gathered at the grave side ranged in age from the extremely old— nearly a century if he'd guessed, though in truth his guess would be short by decades—to the very young, as in the case of a toddling child held lovingly in its mother's slim, pale hands. Their features were distinct, though in some were the signs of relation. Their hair was dark or it was light, likewise their eyes. Their clothes were well-kept, but faded, like a photograph left out in the sun for too long. All were quiet, almost unnaturally so, as if they weren't really there at all.

Kirby said, "When the wizard let loose his plague, his was the largest home in the area. Many stories tall, you could see it from anywhere. Though even when it was new, it looked old, felt old. My grammy told me once that it had looked like the kind of place where the end of the world might start."

Alfred looked around him, and said, "She was right."

"Yah. She was. When the ones who were left decided to rebuild, rather than fixing what was broken, they decided it would be easier to pave over what had gone before. Better to forget about all that death and suffering, like it'd never happened. And so that's just what they did. They paved while we dug, and by the time we'd come up for air, the sky was so much concrete and steel. They'd closed the lid on us, but nothing lasts forever.

"Because, y'see, the wizard's house was still standing, every cursed foot and story of it. They couldn't take it down. They tried. We tried, but no matter what we did, those that came with hammers and fire died, and that...*house* stood. Stood right up into our sky, and jabbed out of their ground like a broken rib. And so they kept building, and paving, and driving their skyscrapers into the bowl of heaven. Until that house was the smallest thing in their precious Metropolis. And that's when he came."

Alfred looked again at the coffin, at the bloodless body. "Rotwang," he whispered.

"Yah," Kirby said. He lay a chalk-white hand on the side of the coffin, not lovingly, not in a sign of reconciliation, but more to make sure that it was still there, that *he* was still there. "He took possession of the house. Or maybe it took possession of him. Though in truth, it was probably both and neither. Though if ever two terrible things were made for each other, it was Rotwang and the wizard's house. And he went into it like the evil seed he was, and in his madness, he dug down, down, down into the old world, and found the body of the red-shoed wizard. It must have been like a great awakening to him, finding those remains. Coming face to face with so kindred a spirit. Like two boats in the night, each filled with the damned. And somewhere in the darkness of his memories, he remembered the myths and legends of the wizard who drug death behind him on his red shoes.

"Through floor and sky he dug, until at long last he made his way here. He entered the same way you did, though his search was much more pointed. You, child, seem the explorer. Curiosity guides you. He, though: he was an invader. We watched him for days while he wandered around, looking in our homes, and sleeping in out beds. In time he made his way here, to the boneyard, and here he found what he'd wanted. Though he'd found something we'd all forgotten, too.

"Legend tells of the plague, and about the millions who died, and for generations we'd all believed that it was a sickness that made men ill, and

Alfred looked again at the coffin, at the bloodless body.

killed them like a flu. But, it wasn't. Not entirely. It killed, yes, but it was also a plague of madness. It struck indiscriminately, and drove those that were infected with it insane. They died, yes, but not only in fits of fevered agony. No, when they died, it was also in fits of raging passion, ripping and rending each other like animals. Like they were possessed by devils of un-creation."

Alfred staggered for a moment, memories of the adults leaving him and the other children behind, driven by an irrational, mad urge to destroy the world that they had known, not to make a better one so much as to watch the old one burn. It had been like watching strangers with familiar faces, ripping down the pillars of heaven.

"We saw Rotwang digging up a grave. Whose it was we don't know. We keep the grounds well-tended, but age smoothes out all things, and the inscription on the headstone was dulled with time. Whoever it was, their remains were desecrated by the mad scientist. He pulled them from the ground like they were nothing. He threw their bones and clothes in a bag, gathered the bedding of their coffin for whatever detritus might have remained, and carried them all to the surface. We stood here, and watched. We should have done more. We might have stopped the madness that enveloped your world."

In sporadic flicks and flutters, Alfred's mind pieced together what Kirby had just told him, overlaying it with what he'd seen, and in short order it was all clear to him. Rotwang, the madman, would-be destroyer of worlds, had drug the remains into the bright light of Metropolis, and in them had managed to free the plague of madness. Putting his incredible, twisted mind to work, he'd made it stronger, mutated it into something worse than it had been, and in some way that he couldn't even guess had injected it into the workings of his creation, the faux-Maria, the terrifying Futura. Then, as she'd danced for his parents, their friends and enemies and fellow toilers, that madness had seeped from her, dirtying their very souls, until they'd been driven to the same kind of lunacy that had come so, so close to killing the world once already.

Alfred looked at the bloodless corpse in the coffin and fought the urge to spit on it. The disgust he felt was something new. Something corrupting. Something beyond sadness or disappointment. In that cold, dead face he saw personified the essence of fallen man, the sinner who'd given up paradise.

The somber silence that followed was split by a blood-curdling scream from the fringes of the gathered crowd. Nearly a hundred heads turned in unison so see one of their member fall, eyes bulging. The dying woman was near the surrounding fence, thirty feet from anyone else, clawing at her neck, at the black metal fist that crushed the life from her.

By the time she was reached, it was too late for the victim of the hand. Her throat was crushed, her body shook in its last convulsions as the life left her.

The hand was gone, leaving a trail of flattened grass in its wake.

"Not again," said one of those clustered around the dead woman. The voice was flat, the owner overwhelmed by emotion.

"How?" Alfred asked.

Craning his neck to look into the bushes and other growths on the far side of the fence, Kirby answered, "We're not sure. When we went into the great Metropolis to drag his remains down into our world, Rotwang's robotic hand was as lifeless as the rest of him. But when we dropped him into the coffin, something happened. Another caretaker was crossing his arms when all of a sudden the hand twitched, and moved, and was alive! It ripped itself from his body as if all the malice that had fueled Rotwang had gone over to fuel it, too.

"We all stood there, and did nothing while it moved around inside the coffin, feeling its way free. By chance it took hold of my friend's sleeve, and drug itself up until it had latched into his throat, and killed him. We were all so shocked that we could only watch. By the time we could act, it was too late. It was gone. We've been searching for it since. That's what I was doing when I found you, and it. Now it's killed again. We need to find it."

"Not just it," Alfred told him, vividly recalling the shadow shape that he'd seen at the playground. "There's something else down here, too. I saw it. I smelled it."

"We know," Kirby told him. "We've seen her, too. It is Rotwang's Futura. She's amongst us."

✠✠✠

Out into the green hued night the searchers went, Alfred among them. In clumps of fives and tens, they moved off in every direction, the cemetery the hub of their inquisitive wheel. Like barefooted children looking out for broken glass, their eyes were on the ground, excepting when sounds real or imaginary came to their attention, pulling their eyes every which way at once.

With declining frequency, distant shrieks and grunts and shouts rang out from the distance. Each would be found to be nothing. A fallen stick; a flat ball from an abandoned game centuries ago, kicked unexpectedly. Bones found in their former owner's final resting places, to be gathered up later. Hours would pass, and still nothing...

Until at last a scream was heard that held weight and dread enough to let them all know that, no, this wasn't another false alarm. This was something real and solid and deadly.

Dispersed over dozens of bleak miles, those few residents close enough ran toward the sound, only to find a pair of children and their parents standing at the edge of an alley, looking out into the darkness there. Alfred would have assumed that those that lived here couldn't possibly get any paler. He'd have been wrong. Standing there at the mouth of the alley, beside Kirby, he watched them, even as they watched something else.

Teeth bared, one of the fathers pointed a thin hand into the alley, and said, "She's down there. Futura."

Those gathered, hands filled with shovels and pickaxes and scythes, clustered at the mouth of the alley, and one at a time entered it. Breathing heavily, truly afraid—a sensation still new to them—they walked shoulder to shoulder, four rows deep, Alfred in the center of them, Kirby to his right and just before him, protectively.

At the rear of the alley, where the brick walls dead-ended at the back door of a shop that hadn't sold its wares in living memory, the shadow stood. Even so many hours after she'd been set ablaze, they could still smell her charred false flesh. Her feminine shape was a mockery, her eyes glowing, like an animal's reflecting drifting moonlight. Casually she stood there, still too deep in shadow to be seen clearly, one hip thrown out suggestively, a hand upon it, head thrown back arrogantly.

"Where," she said, her voice frizzy and droning, "Where is my lover? Where is my creator? Where is his blessed right hand?"

"Monster," someone managed to whisper, before she abruptly launched herself over their stunned heads, landing behind them in a crouch, and setting off in a dead run toward the cemetery. The sounds of her rushing feet were unnatural, like hobnails driven into bare heels.

In a rush, they'd turned and followed, shouting for any who could hear them. Their bloodlust piqued as more and more drew close to them. They ran after a thing that had never lived, yet were still intent on murdering. Caught up in the same red haze, Alfred grabbed a loose cobblestone from where it stood out in the road, and screamed as he went along. In the back of his adolescent mind, he wondered if this was what his mother had felt, or his father, or any of the others driven mad by the gyrations of this mechanical plague bringer when she'd danced for them? But that was the back of his mind, and at that moment rational thought had been shunted, to be replaced by a near-mantra: *catch, crush, kill, catch, crush, kill…*

Steadily ahead of the mob that pursued, Futura made the wide gate before any of her pursuers, vanishing for long moments behind hills and headstones, shouting joyously for no ears save her own. Furious, angry with themselves for losing their prey, the mob rushed and searched, and if the graves had been opened, they'd have thrown remains hither and tither with no regard to their many lifetimes as caretakers of this sad, sacred place.

When at last they found her, the rage and hate and bloodlust left them as abruptly as it had come. The madness died in its cradle. Because she was not committing acts of atrocity, but was kneeling, head bowed, before the casket of her maker. One of her arms was splayed across his corpse. The other hand was holding the robotic hand of Rotwang, found somewhere along the way, lovingly, as it in turn caressed her charred cheek.

In the full misting light of the cemetery, they got their first full look at dreaded Futura, and rather than being terrified or sickened, they were each of them overwhelmed with sadness and pity. Because here was not a monster, some wicked thing from the darkest nightmare. Here, rather, was a pitiful child, birthed by an abusive man, one who'd made her to hate and destroy, not to love and cherish. But there she was, the abused child, the abandoned refuse, never programmed to possess a conscience, but developing a sort of one, nevertheless.

She stood, not consciously ignoring them, but simply uncaring. From her metal frame hung the remnants of false life. The black-charred flesh and burnt tatters of a dress. Her true face, revealed to them for the first time, was not the lovely Maria, but a smooth slate, all but featureless, with expressionless eyes that looked more numb than false. A madman's vision of the perfect mate, Rotwang's model of his lost Hel, his soulless Futura, his perfectly obedient slave, created from purest hate. Yet, in her own unfathomable way, she'd loved. And of all the worthy creatures of the world, she'd loved one of the few, truly unworthy blasphemies alive.

With careful fingers, the mockery of a woman placed the robotic hand of her creator in its place across his chest, then took the lid of the coffin and nailed it in place, using her fists as hammers. Jumping down into the hole that the caretakers had dug for him, she took hold of Rotwang's coffin and pulled it in with her. With great sweeping armfuls, she drug the dirt in on top of them, only stopping when some of those that watched took hold of their shovels and started filling the hole themselves. Almost gratefully, she stopped her work, and lied down atop the coffin, and did not move, even as the hole was filled in, forever burying her with her maker, her master, the architect of her short reign of terror.

Dropping his cobblestone to the grass as he made his slow way to the mound of dirt, Alfred looked down at the grave, and felt for the first time that he understood what the caretakers were doing here. What they'd done for as long as any of them could remember, and further back, still. They weren't watching over the dead. No. They were keeping a memory. An endless memory of things that had happened, and were happening, and would happen from now until the last man and woman drew breath. They were historians. And the cemetery was their work.

In the library, he'd seen the steady, endless task of one or more of the caretakers as they'd copied book after book, preserving the memory of it. He'd seen the love that had gone into every line they'd down on paper. As he'd passed through the town, the alleys and houses, he'd seen how much at least the shells of the lives that had been lost to the plague had been preserved. Buildings that by all rights should have fallen to complete ruin were kept habitable, even though all that filled them were ghosts.

He understood. He sensed the purpose of what they did, even if some of it had been lost on the caretakers themselves. They were keeping a memory alive.

Slowly, the crowd drifted away, to their homes or their tasks, in the end leaving only a handful of diggers to bury those that had been lost to Rotwang's malevolent hand, Kirby, and Alfred. Cautiously, the older caretaker placed a hand on the child's shoulder, and said, "We should be getting you back. After all, child, you shouldn't be here."

"But," Alfred began, then paused to gather his thoughts. "But what if I do? What if this is the place for me?"

"But your people are in the light."

"No, no they're not. They never have been. It's our *brothers* who live in the light. We wallow in shadows, doing nothing but dying for the great machines. But they're gone now. Destroyed when the plague of madness overcame them. If there ever was something up there for me, it's gone now."

"But someone will miss you, I'm sure."

"My sister, Brigitte, maybe. If she even remembers me after all of this. By now they must all think that I drowned. I wonder if... if maybe it'd be better if they still thought that. A clean break for all of us."

Kirby was quiet for a moment.

"I'll bargain with you," he said after a time. "You made it down here once already. Do you think you could do it again?"

"I'm sure I could."

"Fine, fine. Then this is my deal: you go back, for now. See to your sister. See to your mother and father. See to your people. And if, after a year, you still have no home there, you still want to live here, with us, and become a caretaker, you come back. And I'll be waiting for you. We all will. And then, child: you will be here."

With a sad nod, Alfred agreed, and it was with the greatest reluctance, hours later, that he'd ever felt that he climbed the last few steps onto the surface, into the light of Metropolis. As he walked the streets and elevated walkways, he took in the sights and sounds, marveled at the groups of people, both those that had worked the great machines and those that had reveled in the spoils of civilization, mingling together, like long lost family getting to know each other again after too long a time.

This world is not my home, he thought sadly.

He found himself taking those same flights up to the top of the Club of the Sons, looking out those massive windows at the endless panorama of the city. He looked at the cathedral and the New Tower of Babel where they still stabbed at the sky in defiance. He looked, and he saw the dip in the skyline where, deep down by the ground, was the house of the madman, Rotwang, where the wizard had walked out into the world with madness and death on the soles of his red shoes. He looked, and he saw, and he hated it all. He hated it with an itch in his mind, his heart, and his soul. He condemned it a with the certainty that every bright light was just another mask to cover the corruption that was the backbone of this society.

One year, he reminded himself, as he descended the steps from the Club of the Sons. He'd search out his Mamma and Papa, and try to forgive them for abandoning their children while under the spell of Futura. He'd try to make his sister forgive him, for her undoubtedly thinking him dead. He'd try to make a go of it, in this civilization that would try to make itself something other than the ugly, hateful thing that it was. He'd try to see this world as his home. He'd try, and he'd fail, and he'd count the days.

One year, he thought again. *And then I'll go home.*

for Naomi, Eleanor, and Iris

THE END

ESSAY:

Fritz Lang's *Metropolis* is a genre classic, though one that I couldn't sit through in a single go until I was well into my 20's. Not that it wasn't good, or interesting, or awe-inspiring in some of its visuals, but because, well: it's long. At two and a half hours, a lot of which is taken up by dreamy-looking sequences that I fought to understand, it was a struggle. Though one that I kept, and keep, fighting.

For the sake of this little essay, I'm going to skip most of the stuff that's been written about it over and over again. I'm going to ignore how big it was in Nazi Germany, or how the writer of the thing—<u>Thea von Harbou</u> , Lang's wife at the time—was supposedly a Nazi sympathizer. I'll skip over just how many different cuts, of varying length, and updated scores were presented, because, again, I'm no film historian, and can only look at the picture as an entertainment. So that's the light I'll shine on it: how it entertained me.

I never had the chance to see *Metropolis* on a big screen, though if the opportunity ever presents itself, man-o-man, will I be there. The sheer scope of the thing, the special effects, the religious imagery, are second to none. The robot, Futura, is one of the best simulacra designs ever produced, clearly foreshadowing C-3PO, and only getting beat out by ol' Robby. The pictures of the city itself have so much depths that you can almost reach out and touch them. A well-produced 3-D rendering would probably be mind-boggling. Likewise the city of the under people has a sickly lived-in feel that makes the viewer feel filmy and uncomfortable.

The cast of the picture is just as engrossing. Yes, Gustav Frohlich is more than a bit of a ham, but he's playing someone whose entire world-view has been destroyed by a chance meeting with someone. That someone, of course, being Brigitte Helm's Maria. To the best of my knowledge, I've never seen Helm in anything else, and I must remedy that, because every scene she's in just dazzles. While her Maria is kind of a dud throughout most of the beginning of the picture, when things start going bad, she ratchets up her emotional presentation to 110% and leaves me floored. Though her best performance, to my mind as well as many others, is that of Futura. So over the top and outright psychotic, she's incredible, even if for the longest time I didn't get what was happening. She's driving the crowd watching her into a frenzy, making them see red, and pushing along a scene that otherwise would have drug. Which leads us to my favorite character in the lot, *the* mad scientist, and star of the show, Rudolph Klein-Rogge as the incredible Rotwang. To say that the fellow does a good job is an understatement. His performance is so incredible that he's become the template upon which all other mad scientists are created. With his crazy hair, robotic hand, and unequaled flair for the dramatic, he's a game changer, make no doubt.

A few years after watching all of Lang's masterpiece for the first time, I still felt that I was missing something, and decided to read von Harbou's novel. Full disclosure, much of what I read has since left my memory, the stories being so close (as I recall), but one thing that has stayed is the story of the house, the plague, and the wizard with the red shoes. As you've already read in my little story, those recollections form the foundation of my tale, and explain (to me anyway) just how the robot, Futura, was able to so quickly drive the under people into a bloody frenzy. It's possible, even probable, that this was already explained in the book, but again, I can't recall. It's been too long.

I enjoyed writing this story, all things considered. Working in someone else's world is never an easy thing for me, as I don't want to insult the memory or intentions of the creators, but I do find myself doing it a bit. Whether writing Doyle's Sherlock Holmes or Professor Challenger, or raising neck hairs with Lovecraft's pantheon, it's something that I've done a few times, and always dread at the outset, but appreciate in the aftermath. This was no different. I had a blast with this, even though those first few words felt especially heavy. As such, I'm going to send out a big ol' "Thank you!" to Captain Ron, Mister Rob Davis, and the whole crew over at Airship 27 for giving me the opportunity to come into their playground.

Y'all have a great day, and be good to each other,

✛✛✛

HARDING McFADDEN - is a Pennsylvania-based writer. He is the writer of the juvenile adventure books The Children's War and The Great First Impressions Trip, as well as the short story collections The Judas Hymn and Making Monsters. His more recent work can be found in Airship 27's Mystery Men (& Women), as well as forthcoming editions of MM(&W) and Pulp Mythology. He's hard at work on his next cluster of stories, as well as organizing a third collection of his short fiction. It is his sincere hope that whoever reads his stuff likes it.

THE SECRET ARMY

GARY LOVISI

Freder Frederson was the privileged scion of the most powerful man in the ultra modern city of Metropolis. The gleaming towers and cloud-high sky scrappers of the city proclaimed the glory of man in his most fabulous city, but the city held a dark secret.

After an argument with his father, young Freder had left the elite environs of his upper city world to find out the truth for himself regarding the plight of the workers who made the city run. Freder delved into the Lower Depths where the workers existed, where he met the lovely angel, Maria; and where he changed places with Georigi 11811, taking on his duty at the diabolical Heart Machine.

The Heart Machine—a gigantic dread device that looked like a giant clock, but it was much more sinister. It was comprised of massive rotating arms that kept the timing and tempo of the workers and controlled the city and it's workers—it was the timepiece of worker slavery. Freder now tended the massive machine for hour after hour, straining and struggling to hold back the giant arms with his last ounce of dwindling strength, fighting to keep up. It was a losing battle and he knew he was losing control. Finally, after so many hours, hours that had drifted into shift after shift, worn down, exhausted, defeated, a mere shell of himself, he finally knew what it felt like to be a worker in this city of powerful elites—where those in the upper city played in gilded luxury—while workers slaved away below in dark mechanical somnambulism.

It was then, that for the briefest moment, Freder realized the horrible truth. His attention and control of the massive arms of the clock-like Heart Machine then lapsed, causing him to be forcefully flung away from the device, to crash his head against a far wall.

Freder stumbled, felt the wetness on his forehead, his hand came away with the redness of his own blood, then he grew dizzy and faint. His mind drifting off into a nightmare dreamlike state of wild images and bizarre thoughts… dreams and nightmares…and then all went black.

"Worker! You there! I order you to stop!" the police officer angrily shouted at Tamar 34577 as he came towards the man with his weapon drawn. "What are you doing here? This place is forbidden!"

Tamar froze, for he well knew that he was an intruder and not allowed here, but after what he had seen...Suddenly he began to run for his life full of fear.

"Stop! I order you to stop!" the officer barked coming forward quickly, now chasing the intruder. He was one of the limited number of Special Police who had been activated and posted on guard duty in the huge warehouse. His job was to make sure than no citizen of Metropolis ever entered this building, or discovered what was secreted here. No one was allowed here except the Commissioner, Mr. Slim, and his chief scientist, Zadag. All others were forbidden.

Tamar 34577 ran for his life in an effort to escape the black uniformed, black booted Special Police officer who now sounded an alarm. Tamar ran wildly with the officer running right behind him. While Tamar was just a lowly worker, he had seen something here that he could not explain and that troubled him greatly. He knew he had to get this information to his foreman, Grot, or even to the Mediator himself, but just as he was about to make his way to an exit and hopefully escape the building to attain his freedom, three more of the large fierce police barred his exit. In a moment they held him captive and then handcuffed him. He as now a helpless prisoner.

"Take these cuffs off me!" Tamar shouted in angry defiance.

"What are you doing here?" the lead police officer demanded. "What have you seen?"

"Enough! I have seen enough! What is going on here? This is fantastic, incredible, and how can you keep such a secret? What is this all about?" Tamar shouted back at the officer, who only smiled knowingly as he and the three other officers quickly led him away.

"We will take you to a secure holding area," the leader told Tamar as they dragged him deeper into the depths of the huge building. They went down deep into the secluded secret levels far below.

"You mean a jail cell!" Tamar shouted in alarm. "I am not a criminal, you have no right to arrest me or imprison me!"

"You are trespassing. That is a crime," the lead officer informed the worker. "You are under arrest."

"I am not a criminal!"

"You are a criminal and you are to be held as a prisoner so that you can not tell anyone of what you have seen here," the lead office told Tamar in an emotionless but stark tone. "Now move along!"

"You cannot hold me! What is going on here?" Tamar demanded, he was a worker and he had rights. Or at least he thought that he did! This was not the old Metropolis of two years ago before the worker revolt—or was it? He demanded once again, "What is going on here? I demand that you release me immediately!"

"Not for you to know," the officer replied as the emotionless police took Tamar 34577 to a jail cell and roughly placed him inside. They then securely locked the door behind him. He was now a prisoner and the thing that scared him most was that no one knew where he was.

"Now stay there and keep quiet."

"Let me out of here! I'm going to shout at the top of my lungs to the high heavens about what I have seen here. My voice will resound above the massive sky scrappers and high towers throughout Metropolis in warning!"

"Be quiet. Save your energy. You will say nothing. No one can hear you, this building is sound-proof and completely secure," the lead officer told his prisoner and then the police left Tamar to stew alone in his jail cell. He was now secretly held, in a secret building, where he had discovered an amazing secret, that he knew threatened everyone in Metropolis.

Tamar 34577 had only come upon his discovery by accident. He had been asked by a co-worker to check a leak in the roof of the next building, and on his own volition, he had entered this building—the building next to it—to inspect the wall between them for a leak or water damage. Instead, what he had discovered here in this closed off building had rattled him to the core of his mind. He wondered how he would ever be able to escape because he knew that he must get the truth out about what he had seen here to the authorities. He had to find Foreman Grot, and also warn the Mediator!

✝✝✝

"The new police are not at all like the current police," worker Georgi 11811, told Foreman Grot the next morning with quiet trepidation, as they tended the machines down in The Depths of the city of Metropolis.

"What do you mean, Georgi? I have not seen any of these new police yet," Grot asked, he was the foreman, and as such leader of all the workers in the city, workers that until two years ago had been nothing more than slaves who toiled in The Depths, the vast dark, smoky, hot underground factory that ran the great city.

"They are there, somewhere, I have been told, but being hidden. One worker says he saw them and was scared by them. Another worker, Tamar 34577, has disappeared. Yet another worker told me the new police seem to do nothing at all, they just stand silently at attention in row after row. It is as if they are waiting to be told what to do, but he was shocked when he noticed that one of them seemed to look very close in facial features to a worker he knows; while another one looked too much like a current policeman. It is most strange. It also seems these new police are waiting for something, or someone, to order them to do something. Like I say, it is said they stand at attention, row upon row of them, seemingly warehoused in buildings throughout the city, some say even within the police headquarters tower. Though no one can get inside to verify this. At least that is the rumor, but at this point it is all just a rumor. What does it all mean?"

"It is a rumor, nothing more. What about the current police. I mean the older men and women who joined the force right after the revolt? How are they?" Grot asked thoughtfully.

"They seem to be working out fine, most are good people, and that's just the thing of it, there seems to be a marked difference between the two groups, the current police working now, and these new Special Police that are said to go to work throughout the city soon. It is said these Special Police are better trained, more professional. I do not like them. I'm scared, Grot, and so are a lot of the people I work with from down in The Depths. Some say they have spied these new police standing rigidly like statutes, unanimated, unmoving, waiting. Waiting for what, no one knows."

"This does seem to be a strange turn of events." Grot commented carefully, for he was ever watchful over his beloved workers since the revolt two years previously, after which the Mediator brokered a contract between the two factions that controlled the city: the workers and the owners. It was Freder, the Mediator, who brought peace and freedom to the workers after the revolt, and the flood that took out all electricity to blackout the city and bring all the vast machinery of the city to a stop. It was a time of chaos that had brought the great city to its knees.

At that time, the workers had been treated as little more than robotic slaves. Thankfully, all that was ended now. Things had improved substantially, and it was all because of Freder Fredersen, who had since taken on the mantle of Mediator; as well as Maria, the woman whose heart had become a beacon for everything that was good and just. Nevertheless, Grot was one who was always alert to the possibilities of trouble and he sensed it now in Georgi's warning.

"Our police were empowered to protect and serve, but these newer members seem to support their own type of operations that I can not understand, and the thing that really scares me is that it is rumored they appear to be replacements for some of our own people."

"Now that is impossible!" Grot responded carefully with his usual pragmatic logic, he felt that now rumor and fear had hold of his friend. "That can not be."

"Maybe, maybe not. Remember what that fiend Rotwang did to Maria?"

Georgi reminded the Foreman.

Grot nodded grimly, he certainly did remember, and now he grew fearful at the thought. He had been assured that all that terrible science had ended with Rotwang's death. There were no more machine-men in Metropolis. The Police Commissioner and the Mediator had seen to it.

Georgi continued with some confusion, trying to figure out just what was going on now, "None of the Special Police have yet gone out on the street on patrol, and it said they do not take orders from current officers—they take their orders from only one officer, a new lieutenant named Dek. I can not determine why they will only obey his commands. Senior Officer Kenet cannot order them, and he is a good man, with much experience. They will not explain their reason when asked for not obeying him, and the Police Commissioner defends them."

"I will speak to Freder, the Mediator must know about this situation. He will know what to do, and if he feels it is something that he must speak to the Police Commissioner, Mr. Slim about, then he will do so." Grot told his friend calmly. "It will be settled, I am sure there is a reasonable explanation for all this."

"That's good, I knew that if I alerted you to the problem we would get some positive results," Georgi thanked the foreman, much relieved.

Grot nodded, went on his way to work, but he was worried by what he had just learned, so he decided to do a little investigating himself before he went to report this to anyone else.

✠✠✠

He was known only as Mr. Slim, the Police Commissioner, but he was also called the Thin Man. No one knew his true name, or if he had one. He had a murky past. Though only two people knew it, he had once been the chief enforcer for the controlling industrialists of the mega city, the multi-towered megalopolis, the glorious modern city called Metropolis, working for Joh Fredersen, the Mediator's father. He was tall and lean, even cadaverous, and he instilled fear and dread in many who saw him. It was said he had been a spy and investigator, and that he could be a violent man, and that he had once done the dirty work for Joh Feredersen, and other powerful industrialists who lived in the upper environs of those amazing towers, and who had once ruled Metropolis under their total control.

But that had been in the old days before the revolt of the workers. Things were different now.

The city had rebuilt since the flood and blackout, caused by the worker revolt and the chaos of those violent days two years ago. That had been a dire time, a time when there had been two Marias—the real Maria—and the false robotic Maria—with each one working their light and dark magic, respectively, upon the workers and the people of the city. Since then, the creator of the false Maria, Rotwang, the mad inventor, had fallen to his death in a fight with Freder to save the real Maria.

The false Maria, the woman who was also called 'the witch' by the workers, had been burned at the stake for her evil deeds. In the process she had finally been revealed to be one of Rotwang, the inventor's, machine-man creations composed of a body of shiny slick metal skin. Not human at all. The false Maria had been destroyed.

The true Maria, the human woman, and her new husband, Freder, who was the son of Joh Fredersen, had since married and were now trying to rebuild Metropolis to achieve the best image of what The Mediator wanted for the city. For Freder had now taken on that role, forming a government through a compact between his father, and Grot, foreman of the workers, that stood for the overall good of the city, the workers, the people, and most of all, the children. The next generation of citizens. In the mean time, The Depths, that underground part of the old slave city, had been cleaned and was much changed now. The work hours, working conditions, and the work itself had become less abusive—even reasonable—so that the slavery of the workers had finally ended.

Freder, The Mediator, with Maria, and with his friend, Georgi 11811 helping them after the revolt, had worked to recreate the glorious wonderful modern city of Metropolis in the image of justice and free men. For all now understood the truth of the Mediator's words—that between hands and head there must be a heart—or more simply explained, that between the workers and the owners, there must be a sense of justice and fairness which only the heart can provide. The heart must allow everyone to benefit from material success. That is the only way that a city like Metropolis could survive and it was that new thinking that had saved this glorious city of wonderment during its darkest hour.

Now a new challenge presented itself to Freder. Mr. Slim, who was called the Thin Man, seemed to be seeking power even above the Mediator, as well as control of the workers, and even the owners themselves. Or so it was whispered in the most secret circles. There was as yet, no real evidence of this of course. Mr. Slim never admitted any of it. No one had yet seen the multitudes of the secret army of Special Police in their hidden chambers or been able to confirm that some of them had the faces of living workers and police who people knew. The few Special Police that were ever seen on the streets of the city were very circumspect and did not overly interfere with the people—they seemed to be there for display purposes only. The original police were the ones taking on the full load of keeping the city safe and arresting criminals. It was an arduous duty but one they truly believed in doing to keep the city safe. Meanwhile, no one knew that the Thin Man had created a secret army of Special Police that were personally loyal to him and that looked like many of the people who now lived in the city. It was most strange.

This was all the result of the contract that went into effect immediately after the revolt, when Mediator Freder brought all sides together to form a fair and just government. It was agreed by all that with the freedom for the workers, some form of police force was needed to enforce the law. For a city without law would only lead to chaos and violence. But Freder knew that a fine balance was needed. So it was agreed that an adequate force of police were necessary, and in keeping with the new contract, the ranks were open to all citizens, so that even workers could join the police. Many workers did join and were currently serving on the city police force.

The current police had come from all classes of upper city dwellers, but also from many former factory workers. And they had done their duty well, working together, but it was pressed by city officials that more police were needed, so the ranks were to be expanded. Mr. Slim, as Police Commissioner, was working hard to add new members to the force, but some said these newer members seemed to have perverted the sense of duty of the current police, and had turned themselves into what was feared to be a private army answerable only to Mr. Slim—the Thin Man. Now Metropolis seemed to be in danger from a new threat of total control no one had ever imagined before. Worse yet, no one knew that Zadag, Rotwang's unknown assistant, had survived the revolt, and was now working with the Thin Man to bring his plan for control into reality.

The Thin Man ruled the police as Commissioner from his top floor office in the massive Police Headquarters tower in central Metropolis, from the very same office where Joh Fredersen, had once ruled the city that had once been his own. He used assistants who did his bidding, whose base desires were heavily influenced by the most extreme of the dread Seven Deadly Sins: gluttony, lust, envy, avarice, pride, anger and sloth. These sins became their bywords. Chief among these essential aides was a man known as Dek.

Lieutenant Dek was the first of those assistants to become a member of the Special Police, and for his loyalty and ingenuity he became Mr. Slim's right hand man. He was known for getting things done. Dek's personal violations of the Seven Deadly Sins seemed to be envy, avarice and anger, which made him quite effective and dangerous. The Thin Man felt he had chosen well in lifting Dek to his present position of power. As a result, Dek was totally loyal

The Thin Man ruled...from his top floor office.

and followed every order he was given.

"Before long, Dek, I will control the entire city, control it with a tighter grasp than ever did old man Fredersen," the Thin Man told his chief lieutenant showing an anticipatory gleam in his eyes at the ultimate power he would soon wield in the city.

"Yes, sir, thousands of Special Police are in place now, secretly posted in warehouses throughout the city waiting to be activated. You will have a powerful army for your use when the time comes," Dek replied purposefully, enjoying the glow that shone upon him from the Thin Man's fierce gaze.

"Good, I am gratified to hear that we are on schedule. Now what of these troublemakers you told me about? Some of them have even requested to see me to discuss the use of my Special Police. I, of course, have put them off. I need not report to the likes of them."

"Of course, sir, but there have been some grumblings. Young Freder and his friend, the worker Georgi 11811, and some others," Dek replied with a grimace, still standing at rigid attention before his commander, proudly wearing his jet black Special Police uniform and shiny black boots. His police officer logo shown in bright silver prominently upon his chest, and a smaller version of the device pinned upon the front of the cap that he held respectfully under his arm.

"Yes, those two for sure, but there are others. There is that Maria woman for one, and even the factory Top Foreman, Grot. I think it is time that they all must be taken care of. They are all potential roadblocks to my moves to control the city. Even old Joh Fredersen seems to have weakened his spine these days since his son has taken on the role of the Mediator. He and the other owners have become much too compliant and even considerate of the rights of the workers. I can not abide this attitude much longer, and should they find the hidden caches of my Special Police before I am ready to set them lose upon their mission, it could become a major problem."

"Yes, sir," Dek replied in an agreeable tone.

The Thin Man continued, "I am appalled by the changes I have seen put in play throughout this city since the worker revolt, but of course, I have never publicly spoken of my true feelings upon the matter. I have been most careful to appear to support the Mediator in all things. So far."

"Yes, I know that, and I agree, it is a shame what is happening, but now that the secret army is ready you can…I mean…except…"

"Except what, Dek?" the Thin Man grumbled with impatience, his cadaverous face showing a grim death's head rectus.

"Well, there are very many of the current police who do not agree with your methods to take over the city for the good of the people—as you call it. They say they will resist your move, so I believe they must be dealt with first."

"I agree, Dek," his master growled, showing some anger at this mentioning of yet more opposition by many of the police currently under his command. No opposition to his plan of total control could be allowed. It must be stomped out before he could bring his plan to fruition.

"Senior Officer Kenet, and Officer Tam have popular appeal amongst the rank and file of the police serving presently. Kenet is older and well respected. They have much support from these current members who had been drawn from citizens of the upper city, as well as members who had come from the worker classes. They openly preach their belief that the police should serve the people—all of the people—with fairness and impartiality. In this manner, they follow the advice of the Mediator."

"Serve impartially, and with fairness? What a ridiculous concept! Metropolis was not built upon impartiality or fairness."

"No, sir, it was not," Dek admitted in a low monotone, for he knew the history of the city quite well. It had been built by slave labor and had become a vast slave city where the workers toiled soullessly in the underground Depths; while the pampered wealthy and powerful played their games in lavish luxury in the Upper City.

Mr. Slim, the Thin Man looked at Dek closely, then as if coming to a momentous decision, he said, "Well then, we must move to take care of Officers Kenet and Tam, and all of their followers, and see to it that they, and all who hold these views, are discredited. I want them arrested and dealt with efficiently."

"It will be done at once, sir," Dek told his superior.

"See to it immediately, Dek," the Thin Man demanded with a grim smile. Anticipating the elimination of these last few insignificant obstructions to his plan for conquest and control of the city made him feel better about the future and his plans.

The Thin Man nodded menacingly, with grim self-satisfaction, for there was something else that he alone knew. Something that not even Freder, the Mediator, knew. The Thin Man had a secret weapon that none knew about that would ensure the success of his secret plan. He had a secret army of Special Police who were totally loyal to him—and him only—and they would obey any order that he gave them. That realization gave him a most warm and reassuring feeling—and soon he would put them to use!

Lieutenant Dek was dismissed to carry out his orders and he quickly left the room.

✝✝✝

"Come in here, Zadag, I need to speak with you," the Thin Man spoke out when he knew he was alone. A secret panel slowly opened in the wall behind his desk and a short, hump-backed man slowly entered his office. It was obvious the man had been listening in on all that was spoken from where he had been hidden in that secret room off the Commissioner's main office.

"Yes, sir," Zadag replied in his usual submissive tone, for he knew no other mode of expression when dealing with the Thin Man. He had been Rotwang's assistant, a creature who had willingly done the bidding of the mad inventor. Zadag was a small man, kept much in the shadows by the great man Rotwang, but one who had learned all the great man's secrets and he used them now for his new master. "What can I do for you?"

"How is the project coming along?" the Thin Man asked thoughtfully, for this was work very close to his dark brimstone heart.

"Very well, sir, everything is progressing according to schedule," Zadag stated without any drama or emotion. He was a cold-hearted man who usually felt more comfortable among machines than with humans.

"Good, now come with me. I want us to take a walk down to the lower floors. I want to see the factory again for myself now that the last ranks of the machine-men are being created."

"Yes, sir, then please follow me," Zadag replied and led his new master into the secret room off the office he had just come out from. Then the two walked down a long winding stairway that opened onto a fenced metal ledge where they could view the many tiered and many floored vast expanse of the machine-man factory. The area was immense, taking up the entire police tower, but for the Commissioner's top floor office.

This was the secret location where all Rotwang's insidious machines and mechanical devices from his strange old house had been brought two years ago, and where Zadag had secretly put together the machines, that ran the machines, that made the machine-men. All done without any human input, but for Zadag. The Thin Man's secret army was being created before his eyes, silver metallic beings mechanically put together by other machines along a winding modern assembly line, then covered with a spray on patina of synthetic flesh-like skin and a pre-formed face, to make them appear human.

This was done through the brilliant light ray device where glowing circular pulsing bands of white light moved up and down the shiny metallic surface of a machine-man body bombarding the cold blobs of synthetic flesh to transform them into a preconceived image. When the process was complete, the metallic outside suddenly was gone, to be covered by a natural-looking surface of pseudo human flesh!

And the best part of the entire operation for the Thin Man was that none of the machine-men knew that they were machines. They were programmed to believe themselves to be *human*. This was important because it is written that no machine can kill a human.

Zadag led the Thin Man down the steps ever deeper into the vast interior of the police headquarters tower, into the central area that he now used as his secret factory. This had become a closed off, heavily guarded area where only Zadag and the Thin Man were allowed. Only a few select Special Police were posted on guard here. No one else in all of Metropolis knew about this hidden factory or was allowed inside. Not even the Mediator himself. Though there were rumors about the factory's existence, no one had any idea of its location.

It had been a bold and brilliant move by the Thin Man to locate the secret assembly factory right here in the police headquarters tower. It was a huge building where the Thin Man had total control. So it was here where Zadag had built the machines and the mechanical assembly line that put together the machine-men he had copied from the plans created by old Rotwang. Here was set up the machine that formed the circular light and energy pulse that brought his machine-men to life—and that had been used by Rotwang to create the false Maria—to make the machine-men appear to be human.

Now Zadag had the machine set up and working to build the flesh-like covering over the cold metallic features of these machine-men, which turned them each into beings who now appeared to be human. Each one made up to look like a current inhabitant of Metropolis. An exact duplicate. The assembly line moved on forever, one creation being put together, after the next. Then the men's bodies were dressed in Special Police uniforms, armed, and finally ordered to form up into endless lines, standing firmly at attention. Waiting. Silent. Since they were not human, but only machines, they did not get tired standing for so many days and weeks in attentive formation. They did not get hungry, nor need any food or water, but stood silent and ready, armed and alert, waiting to follow whatever orders they were given once activated by the Thin Man.

The Thin Man looked out upon the endless rows of stern-faced machine creatures, creatures who appeared to be so human, and would do his every bidding, and even he was impressed. The ranks of them seemed to go on forever, row upon row, line upon line, there were thousands of them and each one looked the spitting image of a current citizen of Metropolis—a citizen it would soon replace. Zadag's mysterious assembly line was cranking out more and more of them with every passing hour. It was amazing, incredible, and the Thin Man smiled with a twisted grin of rattle-snake-eyed danger.

"My army is almost ready!" the Thin Man shouted allowing a malevolent joy to seize him momentarily.

"Yes, sir, there are hundreds of them now, thousands of them actually," Zadag stated calmly. "They will be unstoppable!"

"And what of that first one you made?" the Thin Man asked curiously. "It was the best of them all, you told me?"

"Yes, but even he does not know the truth of his origin. He was created from me, in some ways. However, neither he, nor any of the others know the truth, that they are machine-men and *not* humans," Zadag replied allowing a twisted grimace of superiority at his knowing of this knowledge.

"And believing they are human, they will be prone to accept my order to fire upon other humans," the Thin Man said in a devious cynical voice, "and after killing them, then take their place?"

"Yes, they will obey you in all things, sir," Zadag replied without emotion.

"There will be a substantial reward for your good work once I have achieved my plan," the Thin Man told the small hunched-back creature, but the look from the man's eyes was not one that instilled comfort or trust.

"My reward is but to serve you, master," Zadag said carefully, quietly, for he knew very well what must be said to superiors—and what must never be said.

"Of course, it is, Zadag, of course it is," the Thin Man replied with his cadaverous smile as his eyes once again looked over the vast amount of troops who were standing at attention, just waiting for him to command them to take control of the city. Soon, he thought to himself, soon!

"You have done well, Zadag," the Commissioner told the short hump-backed inventor with a regal nod of his head.

Zadag showed his acknowledgement, giving out a similar twisted grin, and allowed a slim hope that his secret of building these machine-men for the Thin Man would not die with him. For he did not trust this Thin Man at all.

┼┼┼

Maria and Freder warmly embraced showing the deep love they felt for each other. They had been through so many adventures over the last two years. Now they were together as husband and wife, and Freder had assumed his role as the Mediator with conviction, bringing together the hands of the workers, with the heads of the owners to rule the city for the benefit of all the people. Such had always been his goal. This miracle city of the future, which had been built upon lies and slavery, was now beginning to achieve its true purpose as a city that existed for the benefit of all the people who lived there.

But he knew there were those who would stop his dream of justice and fairness for all citizens from coming true. His wife, Maria, knew it as well.

"Freder, I am afraid that it is the same as it has always been in this old world. The Seven Deadly Sins, they haunt our city and our people still, my love," Maria told her husband as they lay together in a firm embrace in their new home, in the upper level of the great city. They were together now and they never wanted anyone or anything to part them again.

Freder smiled at her, then added, "Yes, it has, but you are correct, we still must deal with the Seven Deadly Sins, they are still among us, and always will, I fear. After all, we are but only human. Gluttony, lust, envy, avarice, pride, anger and sloth will always appeal to certain people and these base desires will rule their actions for the worse."

"I fear you are right, my love," Maria told her husband sadly.

"And yet, some of these sins do seem more dangerous than others, and it is three of them that I fear the most," Freder stated. "Anger, envy, avarice, these could turn men's hearts, turn them deadly against us all."

Maria looked carefully at her husband, pursed her lips with a brave look of determination tinged by sadness, "You are concerned that Senior Officer Kenet, and Officer Tam suspect that there is some problem brewing with the police?"

"I do. But I do not fear the police; I fear the leader of the police, the Commissioner, Mr. Slim. He who some call the Thin Man. I never liked him, never trusted him. You know, it is said he did work for my father, but my father will not speak of anything since his stroke. And Josepfat has disappeared. They are the only two people who know the truth of the Thin Man."

"And yet it was you, as Mediator, who allowed for his control of the police as Commissioner," Maria stated in a thoughtful tone.

"I did. We need the police, we need a force of law enforcers, and men like Officers Kenet and Tam, do the job a great justice. They see the police as being a power for good in the city, to serve the people. Much as I do."

"And Mr. Slim, this Thin Man?" Maria asked her husband.

Freder only shook his head thoughtfully. "I am not sure."

"Then why did you appoint him to the position?" Maria continued with care.

"I had no choice in the matter. I had to appoint him, to mollify the owners and upper level citizens who approved of his stern position on law and order. They all demanded I appoint him. After the worker revolt they feared the city would devolve into chaos. So I had to ameliorate their fears. A position, by the way, I also agree on, at least in principle. Particularly after the revolt and the flood, Metropolis needed the law more than ever. Now I fear, I may have made a grievous error."

"How so?" she asked curious.

"I am not sure. Mr. Slim always speaks words I agree with in public, but I suspect he believes something far different in private. I fear he desires the police to become the masters of the people, maybe even ruling the people. He does not see the police as the servants of the people—but as their masters."

"And it is he who rules the police," Maria well stated the reality and the danger. "So he will be their master."

"Yes, my love, it is that in the nub. Officers Kenet and Tam have told me that Mr. Slim is using his chief officer, Lieutenant Dek—who was his first new recruit on the force—to form up some kind of squad of Special Police that will take over policing the city when he gives the word. They are to be better trained professional police."

"Do you believe that?" Maria asked dubiously.

"I am not sure what I believe, my love."

"And what of the current police?" Maria asked with concern.

"I have heard that they will be retired, to make way for those new more professional officers," Freder replied with a sad shake of his head.

"When will this happen?" Maria asked in deep concern now.

Freder looked at his lovely young wife with pursed lips and a cynical glint to his eyes, "I assume once he has discredited me, as the Mediator, because I strongly oppose this action. I have been his one roadblock for months now on his implementing this plan. I believe he will cause some event to happen that will make the people and workers will not respect my advice any longer. And then he will set his creatures, like this Dek, to arrest and imprison all opposition."

"That is terrible, you must stop him," Maria said firmly, unable to keep the twinge of fear from her voice.

"Yes, I must stop him, but it is easier said than done without hard evidence. I realize now that we have been placed in a situation of severe danger and time is running out. I fear that that danger will be on the way even sooner than we can imagine now."

✝✝✝

Senior Police Officer Kenet, and Sub-Officer Tam, along with many others on the force were meeting with their followers to talk over the problem within the ranks. These were the current police—not those brought in by Mr. Slim, or officers like Dek. These officers were disturbed by recent rumors they had heard of changes coming to the city police force.

"These new police, I am not sure about them. There are so many now, and I do not know where they come from, or where they reside," Tam spoke up firmly, carefully, but all there could see the concern that was evident in his voice and features. He was stressed, nervous. "They do not seem to be recruited from Upper City people, nor from any of the worker classes, as we have all been. They seem to be a breed unto themselves and appear rather cold and always aloof as I have seen from the few posted as guards at headquarters. The few that are posted there follow the letter of the law, so far, but they seem to only obey Mr. Slim, or this Lieutenant Dek, and I do not like that."

"They seem a danger, if you ask me!" an unknown voice shouted loudly from the group, there were hundreds of city police attending this meeting.

"They are still police, just as we are," Officer Kenet spoke up forcefully. He was well respected by all the men and women there, seen as a steady hand. "We will work this out with the Commissioner, and if necessary, with the Mediator."

"Work it out with Mr. Slim, with the Thin Man? I do not believe it!" another voice called out in anger, and it was joined by other voices in loud agreement.

"Come now, brothers and sisters," Officer Tam called out for the crowd to remain calm and quiet down. "We are here to discuss this problem with care and calm deliberation."

There were nods of approval and grudging voices of agreement.

"That is better. Now we are all here tonight because we agree the job of the police is to protect and serve the people of Metropolis. Since the Mediator has ruled us, he has brought both parts of the Upper City and the Depths together, workers are even now allowed to become police. Many of you have come to the job from the factory, and you have done well. We are proud of you all." Senior Officer Kenet spoke up allowing his pride of them to show in his voice and his features.

Officer Tam nodded his agreement; his youth was a beacon for many of the younger recruits—both male and female. But not the newest.

"Mr. Slim is our police commissioner, and as such is our leader, but the Mediator is a higher authority and he wants us to serve the people. Not rule them! Where the desires of Mr. Slim and the Mediator come into conflict, we must always come down on the side of Freder, the Mediator!" Officer Kenet spoke firmly.

There were cheers of agreement and all there spoke up in support of Kenet's proposal. The huge hall had become rather noisy.

It was then that the raid began!

Suddenly hundreds of new Special Police shock troops quickly entered the hall from every entrance, blocking the attendees, herding them together, quickly disarming them, and placing all of them under arrest. Kenet and Tam pleaded with their brothers and sisters not to resist. Kenet felt this would all be worked out eventually, and that to resist now would cause needless violence. He wanted to avoid that at all costs.

Tam was not so sure about what was happening especially when he was shocked to discover that one of the new police looked just like him! The man

"We are here to discuss the problem..."

wore his face! It was uncanny. Some kind of doppelganger, and it terrified him. Tam looked quickly around the room and noticed others of these new police and some of them looked just like men who were there at the meeting. This could not be happening! There could not be two of the same man! Tam quickly moved off away from the crowd. The entire raid and arrest procedure had been done quickly and most efficiently and it seemed that the net had been pulled in tightly and that no one had escaped. Or so it seemed.

Senior Officer Kenet was brought forward before Lieutenant Dek, who told the older officer, "You have advocated open revolt and unlawful action against our leader, The Commissioner, Mr. Slim. That changes everything now. I place you and all these rebellious traitors under arrest. You are no longer police officers of Metropolis. You are stripped of your authority, and are now criminals and shall be judged accordingly."

"You are the true criminal here, Dek! You and your men are breaking the law by this action; this assembly is lawful and just. We are within our rights! Your actions against us are not, they are a disgrace!" Kenet stated boldly.

"We shall see about that!" Dek growled in anger.

"Wait until I tell Mr. Slim about this, he will set things right!" Kenet warned his captor.

"Mr. Slim? Who do you think gave me my orders, you old fool! Take them away!" Lieutenant Dek ordered his men. "Take them all away!"

"You will pay for this!" Kenet shouted as he and his followers were taken out of the chamber in cuffs and chains. Kenet's older eyes looked around to try to find his young friend, Tam, but he could see hide nor hare of him in the large milling crowds of blue and black uniforms. He hoped his friend was safe. Then Kenet and his followers were taken away to the prison cells located down in the underground lowest Depths of the city.

✛✛✛

Police Officer Tam frantically ran through the streets of the upper levels of the golden city of Metropolis like the devil himself was after him. He had just gotten the shock of his life, not only escaping the raid, but seeing that new police officer who looked exactly like him. It was him! It was scary. What was going on here?

Metropolis shone with glorious sky scrappers, wonderfully tall towers, gleaming bright glass and metal structures that reflected the sunlight during the day, and the moonlight during the night. It was a marvelous exciting city, but young Tam did not notice any of that this night. Instead he was fleeing for his life, but he was also on a mission, on the way to the home of Maria and Freder. He knew that he must speak to the Mediator at once about what had been done this night by Dek and his Special Police squads against Kenet and his followers, and what he had seen—these new police who had the faces of current citizens. Including himself! The battle that was rumored and whispered about among the police for so long seemed to be in progress now and it threatened to become a full scale war—perhaps even a civil war—that might effect all the people of Metropolis. Officer Tam knew that he must speak to the Mediator about this at once!

✠✠✠

"It is Sub-Officer Tam," Maria told her husband nervously, for the man was clearly tense and agitated when he appeared at their home. "He is at the front door now, winded and very much alarmed by something."

Freder nodded, "Then it has begun."

Quickly Freder ran through the house with Maria at his heels, to meet the policeman at the front door to their home.

"Mediator," Officer Tam spoke out in a rasping breath.

"What is it, Sub-Officer Tam?" Freder asked carefully, as he and Maria brought the man into their home and tried to calm him down so he could speak clearly. It was obvious he was greatly disturbed.

"Senior Officer Kenet and all of his followers, we were having a meeting, peaceful, lawful, when we were set upon and taken prisoner by squads of Special Police. They said they were under orders. I was the only one to escape, so I ran here to warn you. They are coming! I fear you are in danger, Mediator!" Tam stated in tense words.

"Mr. Slim—The Thin Man?" Freder asked thoughtfully.

"I do not know, but it was his creature, Lieutenant Dek, who commanded the troops," Tam stated simply. He was getting his wind back and that was only allowing his rage and anger to grow at the injustice of what he had just seen done. He also feared for his friend, Kenet, and all the others. Where were they? What was happening to them?

Freder nodded gravely, "I see, then I must call the workers and the factory owners together and we must have it out with Mr. Slim, before things become worse."

"You must act quickly, sir, for the goon squads run by Dek are on the loose even now moving throughout the city. With Kenet and his police allies captured or imprisoned, there is nobody to stop Dek and this Thin Man from arresting you and Maria, and also Georgi and Grot—even your father!"

"He wouldn't dare!" Freder growled.

"He would dare all that, and more, sir!" Tam advised, then added, "And there is more. There is a strange thing I have noticed. Many of these new police have the exact faces of some of our citizens. I even saw one who looked exactly like me!"

"I see, then it is even worse than I thought. They obviously plan to replace the current police, and certain leading citizens, with their own people. I wonder if they have a copy of myself, or my beloved Maria? If they do, they will come here to arrest us," Freder spoke up.

"Arrest us for what?" Maria asked boldly, "We have done nothing wrong!"

"That does not matter any longer, I fear," Tam spoke up anxiously, in dire warning. "They will make up a reason, if need be. Quickly, you must escape and get away from here as soon as possible!"

Suddenly a loud powerful voice from outside the house was heard through some kind of amplification device.

"Freder Fredersen! Mr. Mediator! You there in the house!" the loud voice ordered from the front of the home he and Maria shared together.

"They are here now!" Tam cried out.

"We have the house surrounded! Come out now with your hands up!" the loud voice from the front of the house demanded.

Freder and Maria could see now that their house was surrounded by black clad Special Police and that at their head was the despicable, Lieutenant Dek. The officer came forward with a group of armed troopers and they quickly entered the house. There was no resistance.

"Mediator Fredersen, and Maria Fredersen," Dek ordered formally, as his men came into the house and quickly handcuffed the prisoners, "You are under arrest by order of Mr. Slim, the Police Commissioner. And you, Sub-Officer Tam, as well. You escaped me earlier this evening, but it is good to capture you here with these other traitors."

"Traitors?" Freder shouted in anger. "I am no traitor! I am the Mediator, and you have no jurisdiction to arrest me, my wife, or any others!"

"I have all the jurisdiction I need now, sir," Dek stated in a calm tone, allowing some formality in his answer. "We follow the orders of the Police Commissioner, Mr. Slim now. The man, you yourself, appointed to his position. You are to come with us. You will be held until the trial—and then—dealt with accordingly."

Maria cried out in terror as she hugged Freder to her tightly, and then the two were taken away.

✝✝✝

"Freder, Mr. Mediator, I am shocked and saddened to see you and your wife imprisoned here with us," Senior Officer Kenet told them as they gathered together to discuss their predicament. They were being held with hundreds of other police in a huge group of cells in the cavernous Depths under the city. They were prisoners, apparently lost souls now with no rights.

Freder, with his arm protectively around Maria, saw all the current police were there with them, all the loyal followers of Kenet and Tam, who believed as they did, and who had been stripped of their badges and weapons. They were all prisoners now too.

"The Thin Man will pay for this!" Freder announced with growing anger, but at this point there seemed little he could do about what had happened. Unless he could get to the workers, there would be no hope. The worker foreman, Grot, was the key.

"We must get word to Grot to help us," Freder told Kenet and Tam.

"Impossible, I am sure he is also on Dek's enemy list and that the Special Police have already picked him up, or are even now out hunting him down. His people too. They may even have him held captive now, somewhere else in the city. I am sure they would see to it the workers and police are kept apart," Kenet told the Mediator.

"Well, there must be some way to get word of this to him. I know Grot, and I am sure he would never allow this—and I am certain that he is not captured. He can not be captured. He is uncanny, too devious a fellow. Even now he may be planning some action from a secret hold deep within the catacombs under the city."

"With all due respect, that cannot be, Mediator," Kenet advised tactfully, for there was no evidence for this at all.

"I know, but I feel it within me, Kenet," Freder stated firmly. "Grot will aid us. Somehow."

"I wish that you are correct, Mediator," Tam said sadly, for it appeared that all hope was now lost.

"Have hope, young Tam. Have hope," Maria spoke up for them all.

✝✝✝

Deep within the underground catacombs of Metropolis, within the huge vaulted caverns and chambers, the workers had all been called together by their foreman, Grot. All work in the city had now stopped, the machines did not run, and thousands upon thousands of expectant faces now looked towards their leader for guidance. He was Grot, and he spoke for the hands that built and ran everything in the city—the workers—he was their leader—

Forman Grot.

"Quiet now! Hear my words!" Grot shouted, and the huge burly bearded fellow's voice echoed throughout every room and chamber of the catacombs, to be heard by the many thousands within the vast underground. "We are here to form up and rise up, and take back our city from those who would place us back in bondage! We will not allow it!"

There were great cheers of enthusiasm, loud calls for action. What to do? The workers were ready. They were waiting to be told what to do.

"Workers of Metropolis, a dark power has taken over the police force and now controls the Upper City and has imprisoned our police and our Mediator. We must rise up to save the loyal police and the Mediator. Follow me to the prisons, to the cells down here on the other side of the city where the Police commissioner, that fiend, Mr. Slim, has imprisoned our beloved Mediator, the lovely Maria, and all good police. Join me! We go now to free them! Follow me workers of Metropolis! Rise up! We must free the Mediator!"

Grot waved his bulky arms in great wild gesticulations that got the crowds of workers mobilized and quickly moving forward. They were a vast but calm mob, walking with firm determination.

The police prison cells also being located in The Depths below the city, made it an easy matter for Grot to lead his mob throughout the lower depths of Metropolis, and across the subterranean levels, to enter the police prison and break open the jail cells and free all the prisoners. Most all of them being the current uniformed police of the city. They also quickly freed the Mediator, Freder Fredersen, and his wife, Maria.

"You are all safe! You are all free now, sir," Grot told Freder with a wide grin showing through his round bearded face.

"I thank you, my friend," the Mediator replied. "I knew you would come."

"How did you know?" Grot asked curiously.

"I do not know, I just knew it," Freder replied as if it were the most natural thing in the world for him to know this fact. "The soul of the workers would not stand for what has happened this day!"

Grot nodded deeply, then asked, "So now what?"

"Now, we rise up, workers and the police of Kenet's band of followers all united, and we arrest Dek and the Police Commissioner—this Mr. Slim who is called the Thin Man. They have much to pay for. Come now, bring your workers, mix them among Kenet's police, and all of you follow me into the Upper City so we can right this great wrong!" Freder told the workers and police who began to follow him.

All there cheered Freder's words of action and encouragement and with Maria at his side, the large group—more like an army itself now—workers with police—followed their Mediator into the streets of the Upper City, into the heart of great Metropolis to march on the lofty police headquarters tower.

✠✠✠

The Thin Man sat alone in his top floor office in the great tower. He was busy working out the details of the trials and executions he would soon order— and then planning the new regime he would soon bring to the city. His city now! He was interrupted in these plans when his chief lieutenant, Dek, burst into his office.

"They are coming! Thousands of them!" Dek cried out showing some fear. "They are coming for us now!"

"Who is coming? What are you talking about?" the Thin Man demanded, angry at being disturbed. "I thought you had everything under control?"

"I thought I did too, but they have united, the workers and the police, and they are here now. The Mediator has arrived with an army of workers under Grot, and the current police under Kenet, who have been freed from their prison. They have joined forces!"

"Fools! They shall pay the price for their opposition to me!" the Thin Man growled in rage.

Lieutenant Dek looked at his master nervously. Expectantly.

The Thin Man's cadaverous face quickly lost any tinge of color that it had ever possessed —even when enraged—and he gritted his teeth in determination. He would not lose this war. It had been thrust upon him now before he was entirely ready for it, but that was of no consequence. He still had his private army of Special Police that Zadag had created and he would use them now. For he knew the secret of their origin—that his police were not as they appeared to be. His Special Police were based upon the machine-men that had been created by the mad inventor Rotwang. Rotwang was dead, but his assistant, Zadag, knew all his former master's secrets and had placed them all at the disposal of the Thin Man. The Thin Man knew that he could not lose any battle using these machine-men when they fought against mere flesh and blood humans. Many of them wore the faces of actual people who currently lived in Metropolis—and would soon replace those humans. The outcome was almost pre-determined.

"Alert the Special Police for battle. Order them to surround this building and to shoot to kill. Kill anyone who approaches this building," the Thin Man told Dek.

Dek nodded, feeling much more confident about the situation now, and he gave the orders to the Special Police who were immediately activated and marched out from all their places of concealment and posted in rank upon rank surrounding the Commissioner's building, the police headquarters tower. They were armed and ready for battle and there were thousands of them.

The worker's army was now approaching the police lines. There were tens of thousands of them now. Lieutenant Dek watched them as they walked closer and closer. They walked with a stern deliberation; they were not a running, out of control mob. They were a determined force here to address great wrongs.

"Draw your weapons!" Dek ordered his police a bit nervously, for he knew they were severely outnumbered by a mob that seemed to be made up of all the inhabitants of the city. However, he also knew his police were well armed and the workers and Kenet's police were not. And he knew one more key fact about the Special Police—he knew the secret that these police held, that they themselves did not even know—that they were not human but machine-men who only appeared to be human. They were formidable fighters, they could not lose in battle, and they always followed orders. Certainly they could never lose any battle against mere humans. It would be a blood-bath for the mob. A massacre.

"If any member of the mob moves closer, open fire on them with your weapons and destroy them!" Dek ordered. He knew his machine-men would do everything they were told to do, exactly as they were told to do it.

The Special Police, many thousands of them, almost as one man, withdrew their weapons, pointed them at the crowd, and pulled back the bolts. They were ready to fire. Then they aimed at the advancing citizens of Metropolis who were walking slowly forwards towards them. There seemed no way to stop the violent massacre that was about to be unleashed.

✝✝✝

"Zadag, you have done well," the Thin Man told the inventor who was the creator of his machine-man army. "You have saved all of Rotwang's knowledge on building the machine-men and have wisely placed it at my disposal. Together we have built an army that can not be beaten and soon we will use it to control Metropolis," the Thin Man told his creature.

Zadag nodded, and the short, bent-over fellow laughed nervously, "Yes, you shall control Metropolis, sir."

"Yes I shall, but you shall reign there at my side, Zadag. I shall keep you close."

Zadag, somehow, did not believe the statement about sharing power, but thought better of saying anything about it. He just nodded and smiled, but inside he did not like the implications of being 'kept close' to the Thin Man one bit.

"Look, through the televisor, see the images there, they come here now, all at once," the Thin Man stated in wonder as they looked at the large video screen behind his desk. "Look at them! So many! A great mob. Why, in truth, I could not wish for a better outcome. All my enemies here at one time, in one place, to be dealt with once and for all. It is perfect!"

Zadag gave a twisted smile, "I assume the time is near to set your army loose?"

"Yes, while events are not happening exactly as I had planned, the result will be the same. The mob is even now coming closer, surging through all the streets of the Upper City, workers and the former police—who shall all soon confront my new Special Police. They will be in for quite a surprise!"

"Yes, the machine-men I created for you, they appear to be men. The mob does not know the truth," Zadag stated with a sly smile.

"Neither do the Special Police themselves," The Thin Man replied with a twisted leer.

"No, they do not," Zadag replied carefully, in deep thought.

"Exactly, and the results will be a battle that the Mediator and all who follow him can not win. They are doomed! Doomed to defeat and death! It is a wonderful day, and upon this day a new regime will take control of Metropolis. My regime!"

"Long may you rule, master," Zadag said softly with a slight bow of his head.

The Thin Man laughed, turned back to the large television screen behind his desk to see what was happening on the street below. The two men watched in awe at what was taking place out on the street in the front of the police headquarters tower. There they saw Lieutenant Dek with hundreds, no thousands, of heavily armed new Special Police who were on guard with weapons drawn. The black clad, black booted troopers made a fearful and stark appearance. They stood at rapt attention, firmly under orders, watching as the mob surged towards them, closer, workers and Kenet's police, walking forward for what promised to be a momentous confrontation. In a moment the two sides would clash and it would all be over for the Mediator and all his followers.

✠✠✠

"Stop! Halt!" Freder rushed out in front of the mob ordering his followers in a firm voice that brooked total obedience. "I am your Mediator, and I order you to stop your advance at once! Hold Back! Halt!"

The mob, which had been surging to the center of the city down through

"Look...they come here now..."

half a dozen avenues and broad boulevards, had all converged at this point to form up in front of the police tower and face Dek's ready troops. But now the mob suddenly halted in their tracks. They listened to their Mediator and they stopped their advancement. Just as requested. Not one man or woman took one more step forward.

Freder stood boldly before them and addressed the mob in a loud booming voice, "You all know me! I am the Mediator of Metropolis. I order you to stop now and listen to me. Police Officer Tam, whom you all know, has given me the most unusual news. Those new Special Police hired by the Commissioner, the Thin Man, are not police at all—they are not even human! They are machine-men built by Zadag, a servant who worked for the hated inventor, Rotwang. We all know about Rotwang! Now Zadag builds human-appearing machine-men for the Thin Man. These police are not police—they are *not* human! They must not attack any humans!"

"It does not matter, Mediator," Dek shouted now from across the no-man's land between them. He strode forward to meet his opponent, his gun out, looking firmly into Freder's eyes. "Surrender now or pay the consequences."

"Rather than that, Dek, you should be the one who surrenders to me. You who are leader of this pack of non-human machine-men. They are not police, and they are not human, and once they realize that, they will know that they can not kill humans. It is a law built into all such machine creatures. So you must surrender."

"I will never surrender," Dek shouted back, then he looked over at his troops, all continuing to stand firmly at attention, seemingly awaiting orders, but it was certain that they had heard the words of the Mediator and the words had affected them. They now knew that they were not human. Though they did not show it, this changed everything.

Dek knew that his police had not been told this truth—for they thought themselves human. He could tell that even though not human, they felt somehow betrayed. They were angry now. He could understand that. After all, he though, if he were to find out that the same thing applied to him, he would be very upset. It was troubling for them, though they did not show it yet. They appeared to be waiting to be called to action against the mob. They were all armed with their weapons still pointed at the crowd, but the look on their faces had now become most perplexing. They appeared confused, sad, hurt—betrayed.

"You see the effect the truth has on your police, Dek?" the Mediator chided.

"I see nothing!" Dek responded in anger, refusing to see the truth, but in the back of his mind there was a nagging question that disturbed him more than he realized or wanted to consider.

"My God, you do not know, do you, Dek?" Freder asked the police leader in astonishment.

Lieutenant Dek shot a look back at the Mediator with a curious and almost fearful expression. "What—what do you mean?"

"You truly do not know?" Freder asked him in shock.

"Know? Know what? What are you talking about? All I know is that you are out of order here and must surrender to me and my men immediately, or pay the consequences, Mediator," Dek shouted back in hot anger. What he was so angry about, he could not say exactly. There was something that the Mediator said that now disturbed him greatly. It was not the specific words that bothered him—but some unspoken implication. He tried to shake it off and repeated his order to the Mediator, "You must all surrender for arrest immediately."

"The truth has been kept from you. You lead the Special Police brought on the force by the Thin Man, your superior. You know that these new Special Police are not human—though they appear to be human. Some of them even wear the faces of current citizens of this city whom they were created to replace! However, they are machine-men that only *appear* to be human. They are not human, and they can not kill a human—that is why the secret of their origin has been kept from them. And *you*."

"What do you mean *me*?" Dek demanded in a shaky unsure voice.

"You know. You know only too well," the Mediator spoke up with great confidence now. His plan was working. His knowledge of the matter gave him a secret weapon that he could use against the secret weapon of his enemy.

"I will not discuss this matter!" Dek shouted back to the Mediator in subdued confused anger. "Now order your people to surrender immediately, or I shall order my men to fire!"

"No, you will not! And you still refuse to accept the truth. Why do you refuse to face it?" Freder shouted back at the police officer, demanding an answer to his question.

"What truth!" Dek shouted back showing abject exasperation, but it came from a fake confidence that he did not feel. He was full of rage now, within a hair's breath of ordering his men to open fire, not even considering the terrible carnage that he knew would follow as the result of such an order—but for some reason he could not do so. There was a far more important matter that was working it's way though his mind now.

"The truth is that you, Dek, are just another one of these machine-men, metallic slaves of the Thin Man, created by Zadag. You are not human. That being the case, you can not kill a human. You are a machine. You are a machine, Dek, a *machine*!"

Dek shook his head as if to deny the words, but inside him he now accepted the truth, in fact he had always suspected the possibility in some tiny hidden part of his mind. His thoughts grew confused, frantic. His muscles suddenly twitched, his eyes fluttered, he fought to deny what the Mediator had just told him—it must be some kind of a trick—but he knew that it was not! For even Dek knew that the Mediator never lied. He knew all about the Special Police being machine-men—though they themselves did not know the truth of their own origin—so could he also be one of the them? Could he really be a machine-man created in a factory by Zadag?

"Not...human?" Dek rasped in sheer terror, refusing to admit the truth. "No, it cannot be!"

"You are not human, Dek, not human!" Freder shouted in defiance, impressing his words upon the officer. "You must order your police to stand down. They must not fire upon the crowd. You must surrender to me, Grot's workers, and Kenet's police immediately!"

"I...will...order...I must order...I am *not* human? How can that be?" Dek mumbled to himself in utter shock. His mind was now locked in deep thought, terror, confusion, torn between the duty to order the attack upon the mob—his duty—but was it just a machine's duty? What about his duty not to fight against the humans of Metropolis—and the Mediator, whom he must obey? He found that his mind and thoughts were frozen with conflicting thoughts that threatened to destroy him.

✝✝✝

The Thin Man growled in uncontrollable rage at what he saw happening down on the street so many flights below from his plush penthouse office atop his magnificent tower. Or by what was *not* happening! His orders were not being obeyed. He knew that he had no choice now but to go below himself and personally give the order for his Special Police to open fire on the mob. There was no other way now. Dek, for some reason was proving ineffective. This standoff had to be stopped. He took a hand weapon with him and placed it in the folds of his overcoat. He knew what must be done. He had to end this, and to do that he had to kill the Mediator, if he could get close enough to him to do the deadly deed. It was all up to him now. It would be murder, but murder and killing did not disturb the Thin Man, in fact, it invigorated him. He felt a sudden surge of empowerment take hold over him now at the thought of killing the hated Mediator, smug, do-gooder Freder Fredersen, whom he detested with a passion. A smile came to his cadaverous face as he mulled over the impending action. He left his office with great purpose and resolve, and walked towards the elevator that would take him down to the street level. On the way he noticed the small hump-back inventor.

"You, come with me, Zadag, I am in need you," the Thin Man ordered, grasping the small inventor by his neck, and soon the two men had taken the elevator to the first floor level where he was walking briskly out the front door of the police headquarters tower and into the ranks of his Special Police. He saw their commander and quickly approached him.

"Lieutenant Dek! What is the meaning of this delay?" the Thin Man demanded.

Dek slowly turned to look at his commander showing a strange gaze to his face.

"You did not tell me? Why?" Dek asked in a low tone that was almost a whisper, as if he was speaking from many miles away. "You never told me. I thought I was..."

"What are you babbling about? Order the attack! If you do not order the attack immediately, then I will be forced to do so!" the Thin Man demanded. He would straighten out this mess – one way or the other. Obviously, once this was over, Dek would have to be punished, he was proving to be most unreliable.

Zadag, who had been forced to accompany the Thin Man below, shook with fear at the coming battle and the promise of intense violence he thought it would bring. He was not really sure what would happen in the present situation. He did not possess all of Rotwang's vast knowledge, nor vision, he realized. Would his Machine-men kill humans? The Mediator said they would not, that they could not, but he was not sure, and the Thin Man seemed certain that his police would fire upon the crowd when ordered. Zadag had never thought this might be the result of his effort in creating the legions of the new police that he looked upon, still rigidly standing at attention all around the building. They were surrounding the police headquarters tower, and the mob was surrounding them, but the mob was still held back a few hundred yards away, and the mob had not continued their advance. One man, Freder, the Mediator, stood out in front of the mob and had them halt their advance.

"Mediator!" the Thin Man barked out, his voice spewing utter hatred now that he was upon the scene. "You no longer rule here. I shall rule the city now. Dek, order your men to fire upon the mob at once! Remove this trash!"

Dek turned towards the Thin Man, and slowly shook his head. "Why? I was created *not* born—I am not human! Why did you do this to me? Why did you have me created?"

"Don't be a fool! You are a tool. A tool for me to use, Nothing more. I created you to obey me – now – *obey me*! Give the order and have all these vermin destroyed!"

Dek looked longingly towards Zadag, with great curiosity, sadness, many questions swirled within his mind, then he asked the wily inventor, "Why? Can you tell me, why?"

"Why? Because I was so ordered," Zadag explained simply. "I had no choice in the matter."

"But why not tell me the truth of my origin?" Dek demanded, though he was pleading now.

Zadag shrugged, "The Thin Man forbad it."

Dek's face grew red with anger, he slowly looked at his superior, the Police Commissioner, the Thin Man, Mr. Slim. Dek now showed a vast hatred that none had ever seen in him before. "You! You lied to me! You lied to us all! You promised us a better world – you said there would be a better world for machine-men and for men once you ruled! You lied!"

The Thin Man's response was a grim laugh that oozed spite and bile.

"Dek," the Mediator spoke up now forcefully. "Now you know the truth. The Thin Man lied to you, and to all the machine-men he had created. He told you he would bring you a world where men and machine-men lived together in peace, but he lied to you all! He only wanted to set both sides against the other, so he could assume control of everything and everyone in Metropolis. Listen to me, Dek, and listen all you Special Police, this crisis is over, you must surrender immediately and I promise you we can still have a city where men, and machine-men, can live together in peace."

"No! Kill them all! Special Police, I order you to fire upon the mob! Kill them now! Kill The Mediator!" the Thin Man demanded in a shrill voice. He had decided he would end it all now in blood.

The Thin Man suddenly withdrew a hidden hand gun and aimed it at the Mediator, but before he could fire, Lieutenant Dek knocked the weapon out of the Commissioner's hand. It fell to the ground many yards away.

Dek suddenly stepped forward and addressed his men before they made a move, "Ignore that order! Special Police, I order you to lower your weapons. Do not fire!"

The Special Police, row upon row of them, strung out in long lines stretching all around the huge police tower, now, almost as one, slowly lowered their weapons.

A wild cheer went up from the crowd of workers and from Kenet's police.

Senior Office Kenet and Officer Tam came forward with their men and disarmed the Special Police – the machine-men – but they did not mistreat them. They did not arrest them, nor handcuff them. Instead, they treated them as brothers and sisters in arms. Then Kenet went to the Thin Man and Zadag and placed them under arrest. He also picked up the weapon the Thin Man would have used to murder the Mediator.

"This is unlawful! I am the Police Commissioner! This will not hold!" the Thin Man barked wildly at Freder and Maria as he was taken away in handcuffs and under armed guard.

"It will hold!" Freder told the former Commissioner, "and your insidious plan to replace our people with your machine-men doppelgangers is finished. It is over! Officers, take him away!"

Zadag, who was also placed under arrest, was brought over to Dek before he was taken away. He looked sympathetically at the police lieutenant and said in a soft tone with some pride in it, "You were my very first creation, and still my very best. I created your from some of my own cells. In a sense, you are me without my deformities, and you are as a son to me. I am sorry I did not tell you the truth behind your origin, it might have given you some little comfort knowing the truth."

Dek only nodded, watching as the real police now took Zadag away. Then he turned to look at the Mediator.

"I submit myself for arrest and punishment," Dek now told Freder in a dry tone. "Mediator, I am truly sorry for all the trouble that I have caused."

"I know that, Dek, but you did not know—you could not know – the truth behind the Thin Man's twisted plans. You, and the other machine-men, were pawns in his plan. What is done, is done now. Tomorrow is a new day and we can begin anew. We need not remain enemies; we can have a peaceful end to this trouble between men and machine-men, if you would like that to be the solution."

"A peaceful end? We need not be turned off, or…disassembled?" Dek asked carefully, incredulously.

"No," Freder told him in a careful tone. "I am the Mediator and it is my duty to mediate a solution to our problems so that they satisfy all who live in Metropolis. You and those like you are now a part of Metropolis."

Dek showed a spark of hope, even surprise at hearing these words, "Yes, I am sure that I and my machine-men brothers would like that very much. All we want is to be a part of Metropolis and live in peace."

"Then it is settled," the Mediator told him simply, with a nod of his head.

Grot came forward then, the burly bearded foreman of the workers spoke up with his powerful voice, "Just as the workers seek their own freedom and justice, I think we can allow freedom and justice for these machine-men. I agree with this solution. What do you say, Mediator?"

"I say that we have come up with a fine solution to our problem, Grot," Freder told the burly foreman with a smile of relief that the crisis was finally over. Then he turned and embraced his Maria, kissing her gently.

"You have saved Metropolis, my love. My Mediator," Maria told Freder in a soft warm voice.

Freder allowed a wry grin, "No, Metropolis has saved itself, and I believe the city shall now be a better and more hopeful place for all its citizens than ever before."

+++

Maria, Foreman Grot and Georgi 11811 breathed careful sighs of relief.

"I think he is coming out of it," Grot whispered hopefully, looking down upon the young man who was regaining consciousness in the bed.

Maria cried, "He is alive! Thank God, he is alive!"

Freder Fredersen heard the voices around him and slowly opened his eyes. He had no idea where he was or what had happened to him. He was surprised to find that he was lying upon a bed, in some cavern in the Lower Depths, with three workers surrounding him with dire faces that were now changing with looks of hope and smiles of joy. Gradually he recognized each of them, even as his head pounded with intense pain, and he wondered just what had happened.

"You were in a coma for three days, Freder," Georgi told his young friend from the upper world of Metropolis, who had changed places with him to see for himself the plight of the workers of the city – and who had been knocked out cold by the flailing arms of the diabolical Heart Machine.

"What happened?" Freder whispered, trying to sort out his thoughts from what he now realized had been mere dreams. Dreams that seemed so vivid.

"We thought you dead. You were in a coma for many hours, dreaming, shouting insane things, having terrible nightmares," Maria told him softly, "but you are all right now."

"All right, now?" Freder said thoughtfully, wondering. Am I all right? Is Metropolis all right? So none of his dreams – none of what he remembered, none of what he had done – had actually happened! It was tragic. He looked at the three people surrounding his bed, "Then…then it was all a dream? All of it was a dream? The worker revolt and the aftermath…And Mr. Slim – The Thin Man…and his secret army of Special Police?"

"What worker revolt?" Grot asked carefully.

"Who is Mr. Slim?" Maria asked curiously.

"And what secret army of Special Police?" Grot added with concern now.

Georgi, allowed an indulgent grin and explained to Freder, "You were hit on the head pretty hard and went into a coma, so you had some weird dreams. I do not know what you saw in your dreams, but forget about them, they mean nothing. They were just dreams. I think it best now, that once you recover, you return to the upper city, and your father, where you belong."

Freder was astonished. Nothing had changed here. His dreams were just that —- dreams. It all seemed so tragic. He saw now that there was much work that was needed to be done to make his dreams come true. Freder allowed a smile as he looked at the three people around his bed, then he spoke in a firm and forceful voice. "Yes, you are right, perhaps that might be best, at least for a time, my friends. But know this, Metropolis must change, and I shall now work to achieve that change."

THE END

ON WRITING "THE SECRET ARMY"

One of my favorite films of all time has to be Metropolis. It has come down to us from the early days of black & white silent films from the 1920s as a masterpiece of the science fiction genre. However, the film version most of us have become familiar with as a science fiction story is not exactly what the original film was intended to be. That is because the original German film was cut, with more than a half hour of scenes deleted. Some of these were key and important scenes to the story. It was only in the last few years where an uncut original copy had been discovered and the film was restored to it's original version. Now this original version of Metropolis turns that science fiction story even farther along into a darker rather hard-boiled noir film. It is a film even more concerned with the plight of the workers and the people of the great city and the evil they face—it also features quite different and detailed versions of some of the characters. For instance, Mr. Slim, The Thin Man; in the cut version he seems to be nothing more than a mere servant or butler to Joh Fredersen; however in the original uncut version he has a far wider and more sinister role. There are also other subtle differences. These make for a fascinating story that expands the scope and power of the film.

In my original Metropolis story "The Secret Army" I wanted to take in these aspects of the uncut film and use them to tell a new story that took a look at one possible future that comes out of the dream mind of the hero Freder Fredersen, who would become the Mediator. It is part dream and part prediction that has not yet occurred. I enjoyed telling this prequel to the film that takes in aspects of the film and twists them around a bit in a manner that I hope is original and interesting to the many fans of this classic film. I believe that the character of Mr. Slim, The Thin Man, makes a terrific super villain who we get only a hint of his true depth, even in the complete version of the film. I wanted to explore the man and his deeds to show what such a person could be capable of, and how he would affect Metropolis if ever in a position of power. I have tried to show him and the other characters in Metropolis, in different and challenging roles. I hope I have been successful and that you enjoy my story.

✠✠✠

GARY LOVISI is the author of various stories that have appeared in Airship27 books over the years, including such quintessential pulp characters as The Moon Man, The Crimson Mask, The Purple Scar and The Phantom Detective.

His latest books include The Secret Adventures of Sherlock Holmes: Book Three (Ramble House); and the forthcoming, Sherlock Holmes & Mr. Mac (Stark House Press, Black Gat Book #11); as well as his popular 2012 Holmes novel for Airship27, Sherlock Holmes: The Baron's Revenge. He is a Mystery Writers of America Edgar Nominated author for his Sherlock Holmes story, "The Adventure of the Missing Detective." Lovisi has also written three books in his Jon Kirk of Ares series, a sword and fantasy series inspired by Edgar Rice Burroughs' John Carter of Mars books; with two new books in the series: #4 The Mind Masters, and #5 The Time Masters, forthcoming this summer. To find out more about Gary Lovisi and his books check out his website at www.gryphonbooks.com or visit him on Facebook.

ARTIST—

JAMES E. LYLE (or Doodle) is a native of western North Carolina living in the mountains near the town of Waynesville. In the sixth grade he decided that being an artist was what mainly interested him.

Doodle has been a professional sequential illustrator since 1983, working primarily as a freelance but occasionally dabbling in full-time employment.He is artist for the Aster Award-winning comic book SPARK, as well as theSilver Reuben Award-winning museum installation, Creepy Nature.

Doodle is a member in good standing of the National Cartoonists Society since 2007. He has served as both Chair and Vice-Chair of the Southeast Chapter of the NCS.

For Airship 27 Productions he has illustrated a number of books including Domino Lady Volumes 1-4, Shadows of Love (by R.A. Jones), and Towers of Metropolis Volume 2.

www.ingramcontent.com/pod-product-compliance
Lightning Source LLC
Chambersburg PA
CBHW070823250626
47170CB00006B/2194